Hugh

JUSTICE SERIES BOOK 6

KATHI S. BARTON

This is a work of fiction. Names, characters, places, and incidents are products of the author's imagination or are used fictitiously and are not to be construed as real. Any resemblance to actual events, locations, organizations, or persons, living or dead, is entirely coincidental.

World Castle Publishing, LLC
Pensacola, Florida
Copyright © Kathi S. Barton 2017
Paperback ISBN: 9781629897578
eBook ISBN: 9781629897585
First Edition World Castle Publishing, LLC, July 24, 2017
http://www.worldcastlepublishing.com
Licensing Notes
Cover: Karen Fuller
Editor: Maxine Bringenberg

Chapter 1

"Master McGuire, your father would like a word with you. He said that he will meet you in his study when he has completed his business this morning."

Hugh wanted to ask him what his father wanted, but knew this household well enough to know that they'd not answer him. Most of them would just stare at him as if he had something in his teeth, but none of the staff would go against anything that the master and mistress of the house wanted. Ever. Not that his parents were task masters, but the people who worked for them were very old world, and wouldn't have gone against them even if they asked them to kill him. Which would never happen either. His parents loved him very much.

Nodding once, Hugh pulled his jacket from the closet in the main hall and slipped it on. He knew for a fact that his father wasn't even in the residence, and that his "little while" could be hours. Hugh had been down this road with his father before. He was as forgetful as he was organized. And Hugh didn't want to wait.

He was easily distracted, his dad. Not his mother, but his dad certainly was. He took being lord very seriously, and did a good job of keeping things in perfect order and done in a timely matter. Hugh thought his father was the best. A little on the annoying side, but he loved him as much as he did his mom. They were both his world, and would be forever.

It was a show of just how powerful his father was, Hugh thought. He had no idea — and he had asked — of what made a man know how to be like his dad was. Just simply a man who others knew, instinctively, was in charge. Hugh had known that his parents, the Lord and Lady of Whimmpington, the ninth earl to the estate, were going to be the only ones who took care of the burg they lived in, because he knew he'd never be as good as they were. Everyone in the house did, as well as all of Whimmpington. Hell, he was pretty sure that all of the world knew it. His parents were perfectly suited to being in charge, while he, on the other hand, liked to just have fun. He supposed someday he'd have to straighten up, but not any time soon.

As he made his way to his car, he thought of what his father might want with him now. He'd graduated from college, as his father had wanted. Gotten the grades that were required of a man of his stature, and he'd made sure that he kept his nose out of trouble and his dick properly sheathed when he did have to have sex.

Smiling, he thought about the sheathed sex he'd had last night. Mary had always been more than willing to let him toss her skirts up over her head and fuck her. In fact, it was a well-known fact that anyone could have Mary for a price. He thought perhaps his dad was the only man alive who had not had a go at her. The woman could suck a nail through a board, too, when she gave head. Crude? Yes. He was no more interested in anything long term than he thought she was. But good Christ, the woman could fuck well.

He'd met her in her father's orchard just after supper last night, and she'd been as naked as the day she was born. He'd nearly come in his pants when he found her leaning against the apple tree fingering her pretty, bare pussy. As soon as she saw him, she spread her legs and told him to eat her. Not one to turn down a splendid offer like that, he'd stripped down and gotten down on his knees before her.

She came twice before she begged him to fuck her. Standing up, Hugh had looked at her, a prime woman who loved sex as much as he did, and wondered if all the rumors about her were true. He'd bet they were, just as the ones about her fucking her way through high school and beyond were. When she'd told him to meet her there, she said she'd give him a fuck to remember, and he was pretty sure she was going to do just that. That was going to be the last time they'd be meeting out here, as he was moving away next week.

Mary had large breasts and dark, thick nipples. Lifting up her left breast with both hands, he suckled it while she fisted his cock. When she begged him again to fuck her and Hugh pulled a condom from his pocket, she told him she was too needy to wait, but he knew that there was never going to be unprotected sex between them. Mary had been around, and if she didn't have protected sex, there was no way he was going to stick his dick in her without a condom. Hugh did not want to chance getting anything she might have picked up elsewhere, much less a child with her. Between long pulls on his cock with her mouth and hands, Hugh knew that he wasn't going to last as long as she liked to go if she kept this up.

"Mary, love, unless you want me to come before I'm in

you, you'd better stand up and let me inside of you." Her mouth let go of him with a small pop, and he wanted to beg her to take him again. "You have a mouth that begs to be fucked. But I need to be in your pussy. Later we can play if you want." As soon as he pulled the condom over himself, he lifted her up by her ass and slammed his cock as deeply as he could into her hot wet sheath.

"Oh yes, Hugh. Fuck me." He did, pounding her as hard as he could as she wrapped around him. "Harder. Harder."

When she came, screaming out his name as he emptied himself in the condom, he fucked her again just to give her everything he could before he needed a break. When she pulled his head up from her shoulder, Hugh smiled down at her when she nipped at his lower lip.

"I needed that." He laughed. "Christ, I'm going to miss you. You have no idea. That guy I'm supposed to be marrying next summer is going to be boring after this. I think you ruined me. Are you sure you have to go away? I could come with you. We could have so much fun together." He knew there was no other man. And he also knew that she would more than likely never marry anyone from around here. She'd been with too many men for any parents to even let her marry one of their sons. People did talk.

"You'll be fine. And maybe he won't be so bad." He pulled from her and tore the condom off and wrapped it in the foil it had come out of. He was always careful to take all means of DNA with him when he had sex. Another rule of his dear father. "He might have a dick as long as mine and know how to use it."

He'd been joking really, but she only shrugged. Hugh wasn't stupid enough to think that Mary wasn't plotting and planning something. She'd been getting her way since they'd been hanging around together, and she always seemed to have something up her sleeve. Just before he'd been sent away to boarding school, there had been a rumor that she'd had a baby out of wedlock. Not a big deal to him, but the community had been in an uproar about it.

But he didn't ask her about it, nor about a great many things he'd heard about her and her family. He and Mary were fuck buddies and sometimes friends, but not close enough that he'd ask her something so personal. So last night had been a farewell fuck between two people that more than likely would never meet again. Or at least he hoped not. He'd keep an eye out for her, but he knew that he'd never contact her again.

When his phone rang he realized that he'd made his way to town and parked at some point in his musings. Pulling out his phone to answer it, he nearly put it away again. His father would not be a happy man to find out that he'd skipped out on talking with him.

"When I ask you to come talk to me that is what I mean for you to do, Hugh. I know that I sometimes forget the time, but there is no reason for you to as well. Where are you anyway?" He told him. "Come to the office, please? I have a few things for you to sign before you leave. I meant to do it several days ago, but I got...well, I got distracted. When did you grow up? Never mind. But your mother and I would enjoy your company for dinner this evening. If you can tear yourself away from the Manchester orchard."

He sat there for several minutes with his phone still in his hand after his father had stated what he wanted him to do then hung up. Hugh was twenty-three years old now, not some kid that needed to be ordered around. Not that anyone had ordered him to do much of anything for a long time, but...

well, he supposed he was embarrassed that his father knew. Not just about Mary, but the orchard as well. Hugh put his phone on the seat next to him and stared out the window. He could see his father's empire right in front of him. The building stood high above any other in the town. A monument to a great man and a better father.

The McGuires made money. Hugh was pretty sure that they didn't really print it, even though there were times when he wasn't so sure. But they did make it. It seemed that everything his father touched turned to gold. And if his mother thought it was a good investment, then it was. People from around the world came to his parents for advice on making more money and how to turn nothing into something. They were that good.

Hugh could turn a nickel into a buck as well. He'd taken the money that he'd gotten from his grandmother and turned it into his own little empire. The seven million that she'd left him when he turned eighteen was now worth a billion and a half, and growing daily. Hugh, it seemed, had the touch as well. Hugh wondered again what it was his father wanted.

Starting the car, he made his way to the parking lot. His father had no special parking for himself, and he didn't have any for his son either. Hugh the ninth prided himself on being like one of the people that worked for him, and Hugh was pretty sure he believed that he was. There was no doubt that aside from being their boss or lord, everyone loved his parents. Including him.

It was not that his parents were easy people, as in being saps. In fact, they were very stern, if not a little...okay, a lot stiff. And very much in love with each other. They had money, but they never stopped working, either of them. And they did not indulge on things that they didn't need. There were no

10

private jets…they all flew commercial, and no boats floated in the harbors. Nor did his parents have a lot of status things in the house. A few paintings and a vase or two, but things they liked, not things they felt they needed so no one else would own them. Hugh loved his parents very much. He thought them odd at times, but he loved them all the same.

"Good morning, Master Hugh. Your father is on the phone. He asked me to have you go to his conference room and wait." Smythen, his father's right hand man, led him down the hall to the long room and asked him if he wanted anything. It was on the tip of Hugh's tongue to ask him if he could tell his dad that he'd not shown up, but only shook his head. Hugh wanted to get going, and getting this over with was the only thing holding him back from making arrangements to go to the States again.

Fifty minutes after he was shown to the room, with Smythen coming in several times to tell him that his dad was having problems and would come in soon, Hugh was ready to leave. His mother had made a list for him last week of things he had to take care of, and another list of people he had to say goodbye to. Hugh looked at his watch when he decided it was well past time to go.

The noise down the hall had him standing. Hugh moved closer to the door and put his ear to the wood to see if he could make it out. Hearing the screams had him pausing at the door but not going out. Whatever was going on, he didn't want any part of it.

The gunshots startled him. They were loud, close even, and the screams were being cut off one at a time. Moving from the door now, Hugh reached for his cell phone to call his father. As it rang and rang in his ear, Hugh looked around for a place to hide. Finding nothing helpful — the room only held

11

a large table and some chairs—he hung up the phone when no one answered and tried his mother.

She answered almost immediately. He could hear the screaming coming through the phone as someone, he thought it was his mom, told everyone to be quiet. Then the gunshots started again, louder than they'd been down the hall. When she spoke, he had to ask her what she said, her whispers too low with all the noise going on around them both.

"Get out if you can." He asked her what was going on. "Hugh, get out of the building. Hurry. Someone is shooting everyone they—"

This shot was almost right in his ear. And when he heard someone screaming again, he wasn't sure if it was right outside the room he was in or coming from the phone. Closing his phone, he moved to the door and put his ear to it again. If he was honest, he'd say that he was terrified. And not just a little.

The silence was both scary and a relief. He wasn't sure if the person or persons shooting everyone was gone or if they were waiting for him to come out. Picking up the phone again, he dialed the police. They answered right away.

"I'm in the McGuire building. My name is Hugh McGuire. There are shots being fired. I think someone is killing the people who work here. I'm on the eleventh floor." She asked him if he could see the shooter. "No. I'm in a conference room just down the hall from the elevators. I think...my mother, I think she's been hurt, and my father isn't answering his phone. I need for you to come here right away, please. I think someone is killing everyone."

"We have cars on the way. Are you hurt, Mr. McGuire?" He told her that he was not. Then the shooting started again, with screaming. "Mr. McGuire, I need for you to find a place to hide, can you do that? Somewhere safe, as far from the

12

shooting as you can get."

"I'm not sure what's going on out there. If I leave here to go somewhere else, I have no idea where this person is, and I could...I don't know where the shooter is." She told him to stay put, but to barricade the doors. He had no idea how that was going to work either, but said he'd try.

The shooting began again almost as soon as the words left his mouth, this time right in front of where he was standing. He could hear the dispatcher on the phone screaming at him, but Hugh had no idea what she might have been saying. Backing away from the door just as it exploded open, he left the phone on, but slipped it behind him as a man came in the room. He knew him, though he couldn't place his name. Someone...he backed up when the man entered the room with a gun pointed right at him.

"There you are. I knew you were in here somewhere. Hiding out like all the rest of the cowards." The man standing in front of him looked like any other person that worked for his parents. Suit and tie, and he even had a name badge on with the magnetic strip that got him into the building. "I'm going to kill the last of the McGuires. Payback is a bitch, and you are going to pay like she did. I'd ask you why you did it, but I know. I found out. You bastard. You fucking bastard."

"Payback? I don't understand what you mean. You killed my parents too? Please, tell me what it is you think we did to you." The man laughed at him. Hugh read his name badge and knew that he was going to die. He wanted the police to know who it was that murdered them too. "Your name is Burton Dunn, and you say you killed my parents. Why? Tell me what it is you think we did to her. You said her...what is it we did to her that would make you do this?"

"You fucking killed her. And now I'm going to kill you

13

too." The first bullet hit him in the leg. Hugh went down, the pain taking his breath away. "This is for my sister. When I'm finished with you, I plan to go to your house and kill all the people working there as well. I'm going to wipe the McGuire name from the planet. There was just no reason for you to do that to her."

"Why?" The next bullet hit him in the belly. Hugh fell all the way to the floor, rolling to his back as the man stepped in front of him, his gun pointed at his head. "Why are you doing this?"

"Because, you let her die. You killed my baby sister because you and your family are selfish bastards and took everything away when she needed it the most." Hugh thought he could see the bullet leave the gun, feel it as it pierced his head. Then...then nothing.

~~~

"Hugh?"

Sander Phillips looked at his client and waited for him to focus. Wherever he'd been, Hugh was not happy about the memories. And he'd bet anything it had to do with his parents again and the day that they'd been murdered. When Hugh straightened up and looked ready to get back to work, Sander handed him the paperwork that he'd brought for him to sign. Instead of reading it over, which Hugh was meticulous about, he laid it on the table between them and went to the window.

"It was twelve years ago today." Sander knew that, and had taken care that everyone that was going to come into direct contact with Hugh did as well. "I guess you kind of realized that was what I was thinking about just now. It was as if I were there all over again. The entire day rolls through my mind like a loop every day."

"Yes, sir. I can understand that." He just looked at him,

14

and Sander didn't even bother to apologize for calling him sir. "We can do this some other time, if you wish. Tomorrow is just as good. There is nothing really that important here that we can't just do tomorrow."

"No. I need to get this done today." He came back to the table and picked up the discarded file. "Everything is in their names now, right? James and Becky Mullins will get everything if something should happen to me?"

"Yes." He started to say sir, but one look from Hugh told him he'd not get away with it a second time. "Yes, they're named as sole heirs to your estate, and Mr. Mullins, their father, is to care for it for them until they reach the age of eighteen. Mrs. Mullins will also receive a payout to do with as she chooses. The rest, the castle and the other properties attached to the estate there, is to be diverted to the burg, and they can do with it as they please."

As the man he had worked for since that terrible day twelve years ago read over the will he'd had him draw up, Sander looked around the room. It was the most un-office like area that he'd ever been in. Not to mention that no one looked like they worked there, but instead seemed as if they were just the cleaning crew or held some other job that didn't require them to dress up. That was, in fact, frowned upon.

No ties or briefcases where allowed. If they had to take things to and from work, they carried a backpack or some other form of carry all. Jackets were the kind that you wore in the winter, not the ones that gave you the appearance that you were someone important. To Hugh McGuire, everyone was the same. And he treated his staff that way as well. He was quirky, as he'd heard others call him, but that came with what he'd suffered, he was sure.

Hugh McGuire was nothing like his father, yet he was just

like him. While his father had an air that said he was one of them, nobody ever believed it. Not really. With the younger Hugh, he was just like them, if you forgot about how rich he was. There had seldom been an occasion when he didn't go out with them when invited. Birthdays were never forgotten, and he seldom forgot a person's name or those of their family. Hugh was a man of men, a hardworking man who had never gotten over the tragedy of his parents being killed.

Then there was his feeling about suits. Everyone just assumed that it had to do with the day that had changed his life, but it was more than that. And mostly due to the men who had stood guard at his bedside when he'd been in the hospital.

There had been five men in suits, all of them armed and none of them friendly. Hugh had tried to engage them in conversation, talk to them about what he was feeling. None of them had acknowledged the wounded young man in the bed. When Sander had asked their boss why they couldn't simply talk to him, help him when he needed it, the man had glared at him. It was their job, he'd been told, not to get friendly with the client. So for nearly six months they stood there, their hands on their weapons and staring at the door as if someone would come in and try to harm him. Men in suits, Hugh told Sander, were the worst kind of people.

But there were other things that made him stand out with his peers. Not just his ability to read a person without much information and know everything about them, including what type of home life the person had, but also their worth. As in what kind of worker they were at a glance. How hard they would work, and the best possible job for them. It mattered little what their education level was; he would know what they were better suited for. And he was never wrong.

So at almost thirty-five he was the richest man in the world, and also the loneliest. Not to say he didn't have friends, but Sander doubted any of them knew the real man. Nor the ability he had inherited from his mother that had given him the boost up when it came to money. The young man could see the changes in the climate of a business better than anyone Sander knew, and had made them both very rich. Sander listened to his boss better than he did his own wife. However, he'd never say that to her.

"This is good. Send it out to the right people."

As he stood up, so did Sander. There were a couple of other things he needed from his boss, but was hesitant to ask right now. Not today, at any rate. Hugh turned to him and Sander just nodded. Not asking him would not get him the answer he needed. When Hugh smiled at him, Sander decided that now was as good a time as any.

"There is that thing tonight. I've already said that you are unable to attend, but Mrs. Bennett has asked that you escort her and Mr. Bennett." Hugh was shaking his head even before he finished. "She said that if...she told me to tell you that if you didn't go, she'd hunt you down and eat your arm off. I'm pretty sure that she wasn't kidding, either."

Mrs. Bennett, like Sander, was a panther. She was by far meaner than he was when she needed to be, and she scared him to death each time she called to speak to him. He was just glad that no one, not even Mr. Mullins, Hugh's best friend, knew where the offices were. He feared the lovely Mrs. Bennett more than he cared to admit.

"I'll talk to her." Sander's relief was profound. "In the meantime, make sure there's enough staff on hand to answer questions, as well as food for them all. I don't want anyone complaining that this thing was a bust. And you did make sure that there were donations from the estate? As well as bids on the things we talked about?"

"Yes. There is the trip, as well as the paintings that were donated. And there are several other pieces that you expressed a desire to put there as well. The bids that we discussed are with the proper people to use as necessary. No one's donation will not get bought." Hugh nodded. "Security has been hired as well, and there are several appraisers on hand to make sure that there are no problems with things that are bought. Just as last year."

Sander knew that no matter what they did, there would be at least one or two things crop up that had been forgotten, but for the most part, things went smoothly. The function was a Christmas fundraiser that had been held annually by Hugh's mother before she'd been killed. The McGuire name had never been attached to it, nor was it now. But they did raise a great deal of money for the children of the world, and would continue to do so long after the people attending tonight were gone.

"Hugh, there is one more thing." Hugh turned and looked at him. Sander didn't want to talk to him about this, but there really wasn't anyone else. "It's about my retirement, sir. You do know that next week is my last week. And we've yet to settle on who is taking my place. I hate to bring this up now, today of all days, but we must settle things."

"I don't want you to leave me." He sounded so wounded that Sander almost told him that he'd stay. But he had to go. It was time…he and his wife wanted to have some time, now that their children were all gone, to see a little of the world. "What will I do without you?"

"You will survive, sir, as you have done before." He looked at the scar on his forehead, the one that the monster had given him all those years ago. "My wife said that if I allow you to talk me into staying she will harm us both. I'd believe her if I were you, sir; she is quite set on seeing France and all those other countries I've been to on business for you. She and I want to see the world, one city at a time, before we leave this world."

Nodding, Hugh made his way to the door out of his office, but paused there. Sander would do anything for this man, as he had his father before him. But the son, unlike his father, was the genuine article, as his wife said about Hugh...a true man and gentleman. Sander knew that Hugh was a man that was also fighting the worse kind of demons, his own self.

"Set me up some interviews for early in the week. Only the ones that you think will work out. I don't want anyone coming here that...that might want more from me than I have to give." He told him he would. "And Sander, make sure that they have no priors before they get in the building, please. I don't want anyone hurt."

"I'll make sure that they're investigated completely." As Hugh left the area and made his way to the bank of elevators that only went to this floor, he asked him about the last thing. "What of the other, sir? I haven't...there is the matter of the buildings that needs to be taken care of, as well as the endowment to the burg. What shall I tell them should they ring here again?"

"My parents loved that place. And all that went with it." He turned and looked at him then. The anguish was there, as it was whenever he talked of his parents. "I'll go there this weekend and see what I can figure out. See if Drew and his family can come with me. I know that they're working on getting their house in order, so maybe they can use a break from all that. Don't tell them where we're going, but that...

19

perhaps your wife would like to go as well? It would be a nice start to your vacationing. Then you can settle up there and get going on that trip."

"I'll see what she would like to do." He smiled, knowing that his wife would leap at the chance to go to England. "I'll take care of the arrangements, as well as any paperwork that the others will need. Anything else?"

"No. Not that I can think of right now." Pressing the button to go down, Hugh smiled at him. It wasn't the best smile he'd ever seen, but there it was. "I remembered about you leaving, Sander, just so you know."

The doors closed and Sander wasn't able to reply, even if he had known what to say. Whatever he'd meant by that, Sander would have to wait to ask him when he saw him next. Going to his office, he went to his desk to call his wife and mention the trip to England. She was going to be so happy. But the phone was ringing before he could pick it up.

"Oh Sander, you should see it. Oh my goodness, Hugh must have spent a fortune on just the wrapping alone. And it's so pretty that I don't want to...I wish you were home with me now. I can hardly contain myself from opening it." He was ready to ask her what she meant when his doorway was suddenly filled with a large box. And it was topped with a large red ribbon. The men who had brought it in just dropped it off and left, not saying a word or having him sign for it. Sander realized his wife was still talking.

"Honey, I have a box here. From Hugh as well." She squealed, and he had to take the phone from his ear or risk having it explode. Laughing, he continued. "I'm to assume that you're excited about it, correct? Is your name on it, love?"

"Yes. Is that one addressed to you? Oh, I do so hope it is." He told her it was. "Then I'm opening mine. I'll call you back when…oh, just open it and I'll open mine. Then call me when you have it opened."

The phone went dead and he approached the large box. No, that wasn't right, it was huge. At least six foot tall and that deep as well. And the width of it had to be four or five feet. Sander pulled off the card and read it.

"'Happy retirement, my friend. My parents would have wanted you to have this. I know that I do as well. Take your lovely wife out right, and when you return, I expect to see hundreds of pictures. Send me a postcard too.'" He stared at the card then at the box, almost afraid, like his wife had said, to mess it up…it was that beautiful.

The large red ribbon on the top hung about halfway down the sides. The sides, just thick cardboard covered in paper, he could see now, were held together by string. The heavy kind, but string all the same. The wrapping paper was decorated in large balloons of every color one could imagine, and on each was his name. He was almost afraid to open it. Not for fear, but whatever was inside would be epic, he knew.

Pulling on the strings that were tied in a smaller bow than the one on top, he watched as the sides fell open and the top floated down quietly. As they filled the floor, all he could do was stare at the contents. This was more than he could have ever dreamed of receiving, and he knew that for as long as he lived, he'd never be able to thank Hugh enough. Picking up the phone when it rang again, he stared at his gift while his wife spoke.

"It's not real, is it, Sander? He couldn't have done this for us. It's too much." Sander told her he believed that it was and he had. "Sander, he gave us a trip of a lifetime. Several lifetimes. However will we be able to thank him?"

The large globe was decorated with envelopes. Each of

them stated a country, state, as well as a city. Each one, like the one he'd pulled off when his wife called, would be filled with a plane ticket, an address where they were going to be, as well as a credit card to be spent on food and dining. A second card had been marked for entertainment, as well as any incidentals that they might need. Below the globe was brand new luggage that was spilling out clothing, as well as both casual and dress shoes. There were other boxes too, none of them opened, and Sander could only guess at their contents right now. This really was too much.

"We enjoy ourselves is how we repay him. Take this gift and have the best time we can." She was crying now, and his own eyes filled with tears. "I do believe that he's the best man I've ever known. His parents would have been so proud of him."

Chapter 2

Drew walked around the yard, not willing to go into the large castle that he'd been brought to just yet. Mac had gone in right away with the kids, but Drew was working up to it. Hugh slapped him on the back just as he was ready to run back to the car and demand that they take him to the right place. He knew that his friend was rich, but this was beyond....

"You could have told me. At some point in talking to me about coming here, you could have mentioned that there was a castle involved." Hugh asked him what fun there would have been in that. "I'm not sure there is any fun to be had here. It's a fucking castle, Hugh. A big fucking castle."

"It's my family home." Drew looked at his friend, then back at the house as he continued. "My father's father's father — well, way back — built it, and McGuires have lived in it since. I'm the first one to have...I don't live here. I don't know that I ever will."

"No shit. I think I might have noticed if you lived in another country in a fucking castle." Hugh didn't laugh and

Drew felt bad. "I'm sorry. I'm a little stressed right now. Were you ever going to tell me? I mean, ever? I was sure we told each other everything."

"No, I wasn't, but not because I didn't want you to know...I just didn't know how to tell you. But something came up and I needed to come here, and thought this was the perfect time to tell you. And what better way to go through my family home with all the crap that comes with it than to have you here with me?" Drew didn't answer, wasn't even sure what to say to him. "Besides, this will all be yours someday if I were to disappear suddenly."

"Don't say that. It's not funny."

Hugh said nothing. Drew had wondered why he'd been absent on the trip here. The man and his wife, Sander and Caroline Phillips, who had come with them, told him that something had come up and that Hugh was going to meet them there. He never said what it was, and even on the long trip here, no one had asked. It was very strange.

"My parents are here. They hang out pretty much all the time. I never realized how much they really loved each other until now. I always knew they loved each other, but they're devoted too. Like you and Mac are." He asked him if they were in trouble. "No. They just...you see, they died around this time of year. It was twelve years ago a few days ago. I have to settle things here, and they're wanting to be a part of it. The burg—it's what we call the town—is in need of a few things, and I have to see to them. Also, there is the matter of my family's things. They need to be taken care of as well. Mom said that it's time."

"Settle what sort of things?"

He didn't answer, and Drew looked at the couple coming toward them when Hugh did. He could see that whoever had killed them had done so quickly, putting a bullet in each of their heads as well as their chests. The mister had also been shot in the cheek, more than likely because he'd tried to get away rather than the gunman making any sort of statement. Even though he'd never met Hugh's parents, Drew knew that was who they were. Hugh looked like his father a great deal, but there were bits of his mom too. And there was no doubt to Drew that they loved their son every bit as much now as they had when they were alive.

"Mom, Dad, I'd like you to meet my friend, Andrew Mullins. Drew, these are my parents. My dad, Lord Hugh the ninth, lord of Whimmpington, and my mom, Lady Suzette, also of Whimmpington. They've been wanting to meet you for some time now." Drew had no idea how to greet them. They were a flipping lord and lady, for fuck sake. "They won't bite you. Say something, you idiot."

"Hello. Thanks for having us in your home." He looked at Hugh, then back at them. "He's been my friend for a while now, but he's never said much about the two of you, other than when you were...when your business was broken into, he told me that you'd been...."

"When we were killed, dear boy. We were murdered. Nothing much we can do about it, but we're seeing to things now." Drew nodded at Lord Hugh as he continued. "My son says that you and your wife are taking in children who have been lost to the world. I think that's a wonderful thing you're doing. I'm hoping that this year our fundraiser will have enough money to put into your bank as well. It was, by all accounts, a great success this year. It helps a great many people all over the world. Suzette ran it until she and I passed away, and Hugh does now. Only he doesn't attend, which I'm hoping he does someday."

"Fundraiser? He looked at Hugh when it dawned on him what his dad meant. "Enchanted Christmas? Your family runs Enchanted Christmas?"

"They did. I just make sure that it keeps going. But no one knows about...well, one other does, but he won't say anything. And you won't either, will you?" Drew assured him that he wouldn't. "I don't want the world to know who I am. It's why I stay away. It would be too easy for someone to put it together with my family, and I don't want to be a target of that. No one needs to ask me questions that I have no answer for."

"You mean you don't want anyone to know that you're Lord Whimmpington the Tenth?" Hugh cringed from the title and his parents laughed. "Wow. I can't believe that all this time...all the times I've spilled my guts to you, it never occurred to you to say anything about this. Hugh, you've been holding out on me."

Drew wasn't mad. He was a little overwhelmed, but not mad. He knew that Hugh had come from money. But he'd thought, like he was pretty sure most of the team thought, that he'd lost it all or that he'd spent it unwisely. He could see now that not only had Hugh done well for himself, but his family as well.

"It never occurred to me." And Drew knew that as well. Money, the lack of or the fact that he had a great deal, meant nothing to his friend. Unlike most people he knew, Hugh and Steele had never let their money define who they were. "Are you mad at me?"

"No. Why would you ask such a thing?" Hugh said that he didn't know, but valued their friendship. "And I yours. But I am curious as to why we're here. There is an issue, you said."

"I'll turn thirty-five in a few days. And the estate has to be cleaned out and managed, as I said. I've been taking care of it from abroad for some time now. But I have to make it mine or pass it on to someone else by my thirty-fifth birthday, or.... A family member is supposed to inherit it, but there...." Hugh looked at him. "I don't have anyone left. So I have to either give it over or ask the town if it's okay that I run it without a family."

"What do you mean, a family? A wife? You have to.... Christ, Hugh, you could have had a wife long.... What did you think was going to happen, she would just fall into your lap?" His dad said he was pretty sure that was what he'd hoped for. "Well, in a few days you're going to lose your home and your ancestry, did you think of that? Why didn't you find a wife, even if it was in name only?"

"She has to love me. And we both know that's going to be next to impossible." Drew looked at Hugh's parents when Hugh walked away after telling him the reason. They were staring after their son as if they'd lost him. They were as lost as their son, it seemed.

"We wanted him to be happy when we had that put in our will. He was to sign it, the paperwork, the day that we were murdered. We thought, all of us, that he'd never survive what had happened to him that day, and had completely forgotten that he had to marry, and even now, we despair that he'll be able to pull it off." Hugh's mom looked at him as she confirmed what he'd already thought. "I think he's come here to join us in death. I think that the reason that he's chosen now, brought you here, is because he just can't live any longer. Not for the reasons that he told you, even though they are true. But we think.... Our son is depressed."

Drew nodded, knowing that they were right for some

reason. "We've talked about it. All the time. He's even given me a list of things I'm to do should his body come up missing, and who to contact when it does." This time Hugh's father looked at him, asking if he agreed with them. "I do now that you've said it. I don't know how to help him other than to be there for him. But I'm afraid that it's not enough anymore. I honestly think he wants to be gone from this world. But I'm not really sure how he's going to make that happen either. He is, as are the rest of us, immortal. We got some pretty powerful magic, and…well, I don't want to think about what he'd have to do to die."

Drew had noticed there were things that he had little control over any more. Very little, he'd come to realize, when he'd taken on a family and a wife. He loved them more than life itself, but they had a tendency to mess up the order of things. He'd been alone too long, it occurred to him one day, and having people around, ones that cared about you deeply, was something that he wasn't used to. But he wouldn't have traded them for the world. That, Drew thought, was what Hugh needed. Someone to mess up his plans and shake up his world.

"Do you know anyone that he might find to be…I don't know, someone that he might want to spend some time with? Or her him? I don't mean someone that has to marry him — at least that's not my plan — but a person to come into his life and shake, rattle, and roll him." His father asked him if he meant for his son to get laid. "Yes. Well, that'll help a great deal, I think. And so you know, I don't think we should mention that part to him. Ever. I'm not even sure I want to talk about it with you. It's kinda…well, creepy."

"Well said, yes, well said. He has a little bit of a shyness when it comes to talking to us about his love life. I don't think he has one. Or much of one." He didn't, but Drew didn't tell them that. There was only so much he was wanting or even willing to share with Hugh's parents. "He knew this girl, long ago. Her name was Mary. Her father worked in town at the newspaper. He might have been on the board or something at one time, but I don't know now. And they owned an orchard near us. I never cared for this Mary very much, nor her parents. They were the indulgent type with her. Never made her do what she should have been doing. Her last name would be...let me think."

"Manchester. Her parents were Bert and Lenore Manchester. I think they still live on the land, but the orchard is long gone, I'm afraid. The Manchesters had money, but I think they spent a great deal of it getting Mary out of one scrape after another. I don't know...after we were killed I never thought of them again until this moment. Mary, I've not seen her for some time. Could be that she has a brood of children living somewhere. I never cared for her either, but we never told Hugh that. She was...well, she had loose standards when it came to men. It's why we made sure that Hugh knew how to care for himself. There were not going to be any questions about her having his child." Lady Suzette smiled at him. "You should find her, Drew. Maybe she can... perhaps she can rattle his cage, as you said. It might loosen him up a little. And we'll see what we can do for him as well."

Drew wasn't sure that was a good idea either, but said nothing. They were his parents, and more than likely had his best interest at heart. He hoped so anyway.

Looking at the house again, he decided that he was going to have to go in. As he made his way to the entrance, he thought of calling Mitch and the rest of the men. Steele and Kari were at his house, keeping an eye on things while the rest of them waited on the new babies to come. Dillon and Addie promised they would wait until they were back before either of them gave birth.

~~~

"I saw your girl today. Well, yesterday too. She's a cat. Leopard actually. I think that's why you don't have any rodents around here." Steele was only kidding, but Drew didn't laugh with him. He'd been calling him daily to ask about the house addition as well as other things, but this call was different, he could tell right away. "What's happened out there? Something...where the hell are you anyway?"

"We're in England. Who knew? But this girl, were you able to talk to her at all? I mean, other than to see her as her cat, what have you done?" Steele noticed that he didn't elaborate on what he was doing in England, only to say he was there. He was okay with that for now. "She's getting the food, right?"

"Yes. We've been putting out the things that you asked us to. The water in the fridge is being replaced as she takes it. And Kari put out some more blankets, which she left behind. I guess she's not the greedy type." Nothing. "Are you coming home soon?"

"Soon. I have a problem and I can't talk about it just yet. Not all of it anyway. I...it's not my story to tell you." Steele said he understood that. He also knew that Hugh and Drew had been friends, close friends, for a long time, and they both knew things about each other that he didn't about either of them. "Can you do me a favor? I'm trying to find a person by the name of Mary Manchester. I'm to understand that she moved to the States about eleven years ago or so. Her parents are Bert and Lenore Manchester, and they still live here on the family estate. I don't know a great deal about them other than

30

Bert works for a newspaper here, a kind of editor and writer for them. His wife used to be in all kinds of clubs and stuff, but now I think she's just a housewife. Or whatever they call them here. I'm doubting very much she does much in the way of housework, but who knows."

Steele wrote down what he gave him. "I don't suppose you know where in the States, do you? I mean, we're talking a lot of ground here."

"I was hoping you could call in some help. I know that you're taking some time off and gave it to the others, but this is really important to Hugh. And to me." Steele grinned. He'd never thought of that, calling in some of his friends to find the living. "And maybe she, Lenore, was in some things with Connie. Flower clubs and things like that. I don't know what, but that's all I have. I'm sorry."

"No, this might work." He looked up just as his grandda came in the room with him. He didn't look all that happy, and when Carlton came in a few seconds later, he knew things weren't going to be good. "I'll let you know what I find out. And Kari is going to talk to your girl sometime today. I'm not sure what she'll be able to find out, but she wanted me to tell you."

As soon as he hung up, he told them what Drew wanted before they launched into whatever it was they had going on. The two of them were good friends, if a little pushy to each other. But he loved them both more than he could say. Almost as soon as he told them what Drew wanted, they started in on the issue they were having.

"He told me that I was out of touch with reality." Steele covered his mouth to try to stop the laughter bubbling out of him. Carlton thought his grandda was out of touch? "And he said that I'm not up on the newest sayings and music. It's all

31

just noise if you ask me. Even the stupid fashion is. Just look at them kids. Why don't they match their socks when they put them on? Is it too much trouble for them? And wear a belt. Or suspenders. I know they still sell them. Have them get a few pair of them and hold their britches up. Who lets their underthings hang out like that and thinks that it looks good? Not a person I know would have been caught with their... who does that? The young, that's who. That's the ruination of the world. I tell you. We need to make them—"

"I said no such thing, you old poop. I said you were out of touch with everything. I never said you were out of touch with just a few of the wondrous things going on in the world today. If you're going to tattle on me, at least make sure you get your facts straight, you old turd head." Grandda huffed at Carlton. "As for the mismatched socks? I know for a fact that they sell them that way. You simply need to let children be children. We did a great many things I'm sure that our own parents thought were strange and uncouth. Just let them go on being free."

"You mean not beat them. That's what you're saying, isn't it? We should just let them go about like they have no consequences for their actions. I'm telling you right now, I think we're not beating our kids enough. Did you know that they'll call the cops on you if you whip your child? Your own kid? Where is the justice in that, I ask you? Why, in my time, I would wale the tar out of my Beth if she'd done half the things kids do now. Ask her if you don't believe me. And she turned out all right." Steele leaned back in his seat to let them remember that he was there. "And schools now. Don't even get me started on the school system. Why, there isn't a proper one in the bunch if you—"

"No, please, let's not get you started on the school system.

I know that there needs to be improvement. But I doubt very much that it's going to happen because you are upset with it. And I don't think anyone is going to believe that mismatched socks are the sole cause of all the bad apples out there. Nor are some boys letting their—whatever you called them—underthings hang out. It's fashion. Can you honestly tell me that you've never heard of fashion? If you do then I will never believe a word that comes from your mouth, William. Never."

Grandda looked over at Steele as if he'd just realized that they had an audience. "He's driving me crazy." Steele nodded and smiled. "You think us funny, son? I got some news for you…when that little girl of yours has a fight at school, who do you think they're going to blame? You. They're gonna say you whipped her too much or took away her pad thingy. And then let me see if you think it's funny. There is no way I'm going to let anyone hurt that little grandbaby of mine, you can bet the farm on that one."

"I'm not worried she'll have any trouble at school. Want to know why?" They both nodded at him. "Because, my dear friends, she'll just turn into a cat, eat the person making her crazy for dinner, and we won't have to worry about it. If there is no problem to point to, then there is no problem for me to fix. End of story."

Carlton burst out laughing. Grandda tried not to find it funny, but after a few seconds, he was laughing as well. The two of them, for now anyway, had their differences resolved, and he was sending them on their way. But Carlton paused before leaving when his grandda did and asked if the people they were looking for were from England.

"Yes. Bert and Lenore. They are the parents of a woman by the name of Mary. Nothing on her if she's married or not, but we could use some help locating her. You know anyone that might know them?" Carlton said he wasn't sure, but he might have a little information on them. "I'd really like some help with this one if you can. I'm not sure what the family is needed for, but it has something to do with Hugh."

"Hugh's family is there as well." Steele sat down again and waited for Carlton to explain. "His parents died there some time ago, were you aware of that? In an office break-in. I'm not sure of all the details as yet, but I do believe that young Hugh was hurt as well. It was an office shooting, I think. And both his parents and a few others were killed, along with the gunman. It's what gave him the power he now has."

Steele knew that Hugh hadn't been born with his abilities. He was also pretty sure that Hugh had a lot of other hidden powers he didn't use. Not just with working with the dead, but with other things as well. Like his ability to see people for what they were, living or dead.

"Where is the gunman now? Is that why they're there, dealing with him?" Carlton said he was pretty sure that the man was still around, but he didn't socialize with anyone. "But he's not moved on? This man who hurt his parents?"

"No. For some time I assumed that he'd moved on. But then after a while I realized that you didn't know anything about young Hugh other than the bits and pieces that he lets you know, so you wouldn't have done it. Young Hugh is more secretive than most G-men I have had the pleasure of talking to. But he was shot too, I believe, that day. I can get you more details should you want them. I do not know his parents, but I'll see what I can find out about these other people if I can."

"I'd like that, please. And make sure that you don't tell anyone else what you find. If Hugh had wanted us to know, then he would have told us on his own. But since I've been drawn into this, even just the little, I need to make sure that everyone is safe while there." Carlton said he'd be very hush-hush about it. "Thank you."

As soon as Carlton left, Steele went out onto the deck that had recently been expanded and a hot tub added to it. The cat was still there, laying in the sun with her eyes closed. He knew that if he made a move toward her she'd be gone in a flash, but for now, they seemed to be tolerating each other. He sat down and thought of his dwindling team, and wasn't all that upset that they were moving on. He was as well, but still helped clients when he could. He had to either hire more to help him out or simply stop doing it altogether. At least as a team. Steele was just as burnt out as the rest of them were.

Hugh had come to their group last. He'd been wandering around from place to place, he'd told him when he'd come to the interview, and thought it might be time for him to settle in one place. Ray had talked to him. Back then Steele had barely been functioning himself, and had deferred to Ray on everything. Now he and Ray conferred on most things, but Steele had taken over about the time he'd met Kari. She had straightened him out on a great many things.

Steele had known that Hugh had money to burn, but he never used it. There were times when he wanted to ask the man how much he was worth. He had also, on occasion, wanted to talk to him about the older couple that hung around with him at times, but it was something that he knew Hugh would be pissy about so he didn't do that either. Steele knew that they were his parents but nothing more. And he'd never looked into it either. Hugh was a good man, but he kept things to himself, and Steele had never wanted to intrude on that.

Ray had taken Hugh in, like he had the rest of them, and declared the team finished. But since Drew had left the team recently, Steele kept expecting Ray to come to him and say they needed to find a replacement. But as yet, he'd not done anything. Now Steele wasn't so sure that he wanted to band more men together.

The cat stretched, then stood and came to the steps that led to where he was sitting. Staying as still as he could, he watched her. There was something very calming about her, as if she knew that she could come at his throat and tear it out should he piss her off, but she didn't appear to be quick to leap at that chance. He was glad for that. He didn't want to join any of his clients any time soon.

Careful of his words, he spoke to her. "I've been trying to figure out if you're a friend or foe to the people who live here. They're friends of mine. I don't think you're going to harm them, but you can't tell about some people." The huge yawn showed him the set of teeth he'd seen on his own wife a few times. Steele had a feeling it was supposed to scare him, and it did a little, but he was sure she wasn't going to harm him. "Kari, she's my mate and wife. She's a panther. I must say, you're a very beautiful leopard."

The cat yawned again, but took a step onto the deck and Steele sat up. He knew that he'd never be able to outrun her should she want to harm him, but he was going to give it a fighting chance if she tried. Steele wondered to himself why he didn't wait for Kari to come back from town before deciding to strike up a conversation with a huge beast like this one.

Her body was sleek and long. He knew that she would be bigger than her counterpart, but smaller than a male like her. When she came up to the deck completely and circled his chair, all he could think about was that he was the biggest fool he knew. Then Aster, his sister, appeared in front of him.

"She wants to touch you, draw blood." He asked her how much, and would he be able to survive it if she did. "Of course you will. You should also know that she can't see me, and now thinks you're nuts for talking to yourself. I have a slight connection to her for some reason, and I can read her thoughts. Could be that she's been close enough to death before but never tumbled over to the other side. Perhaps when she was converted."

Steele looked at the cat who was standing right in front of him, her mouth inches from his knees. Putting out his hand, he wasn't surprised to see it trembling, and when she leaned to it and licked his finger, he thought for sure he was a dead man.

"Let her bite you. It will be a way for her to communicate with you while she's in this form. And so you know, she's more afraid of you than you are of her. Not just afraid, but she's...I think she's terrified that you're going to turn her in to someone that she doesn't want to find her. But I could be wrong."

Steele wouldn't harm her simply because she'd done nothing to the people who he loved, so he nodded to the cat. He had no idea what he expected. Her to bite his fingers off for sure. At the very least for her to tear into his wrist and let him bleed out while she watched. But her teeth sank into his finger, almost like a prick of a pin. When she backed from him, he looked down at the tiny wound, then at her again.

You should see your face right now. He leaned back in his chair and stared at her as she continued talking to him. *You honestly thought I was going to hurt you, didn't you? I may be an animal, but I'm not a monster. At least not to those who haven't done anything to me. Where are the people that usually live here? I haven't seen them for a few days.*

"They're in England. A friend of ours is having some issues and they're helping him." Her entire body stiffened, and he looked around for whatever had scared her. "Is someone coming? What is it?"

Why England? He told her that a friend of theirs, his as well, had lived there long ago. *But you don't know anything... where in England are they? I mean, it's a big country.*

"It is. Perhaps I can answer your question if you answer a few of mine. I will tell you that I don't know a great deal about why they're there, but I'll be willing to trade answer for answer with you. Deal?" She just looked out over the woods, and he was afraid that she'd go there and no one would see her again. "I swear to you that no one will know that we've talked."

She turned to look at him then. Her eyes, he just noticed, were blue...startling blue like the lakes around his home. And she had a look of intelligence. He had no idea why that thought popped into his head, but he'd bet anything she was well read and smart.

Your mate will. And I'm pretty sure she's not going to be happy when she finds out that I've marked you in a way. He didn't know, but would talk to Kari and see if they could work it out. *You ask the first question and I'll decide if I want to answer it or not. I'm not going to tell you much in the way of personal information, so you might as well skip those if you want any answers at all.*

"All right. Just the one though. What's your first name? Mine is Steele, Steele Bennett, by the way, and my wife is Kari. We have a daughter too, her name is Aster." She said nothing, but looked around the deck and beyond the yard. When she turned back to him, he knew that she wasn't going to answer him.

There is a woman that lives here that calls me Peach. She...there was a time once not long ago that she caught me off guard and I told her that. That'll be okay for now. It wasn't with him, but he was trying to get answers, not piss her off. *Where in England have they gone?*

"As I said, I don't know. They left here three days ago, and according to Drew, it'll be another couple before they return." She watched him carefully and he waited for her to call him a liar. But she only nodded and laid down on the deck, seemingly bored with the whole thing. "Are you hiding from someone that comes from England?"

Sort of. As far as trading off questions for answers, they weren't getting very far. *There was a man once, his name was Lord Whimmpington. His family was...I knew him long ago, when we were children. We never ran in the same circles or anything, but I did wonder if it was in that area where I'm from.*

"I'm sorry. I don't know who that is. Is he trying to kill you?" She told him he was dead as far as she knew. "I have some people that I know that can help you locate his ghost if you want. They have some pretty good connections when it comes to that. Would you like for me to have them look for him?"

Ghost? I don't know anything about that. But you would, wouldn't you? No. But thank you. She knew what he was, not that he should have been surprised. She did trust him very quickly, he thought. *My family and his, this dead man I was referring to, we were never close, but he knew my brother a little. Long ago. Then something happened to him and my father passed away. My mom and I moved here where it was.... Then she passed not long after we arrived. I've been alone for a long time.*

"And you ended up here, why?"

She stood up then, the hair on her body standing as well, just as he heard the crunch of tires in the driveway. Before he could tell her that it was all right, that it was his wife, she was gone. The leap into the yard took her nearly to the barn, then she disappeared inside it. But when she paused, her face just peeking out of the doorway, he had a feeling that she was keeping an eye on him, and Steele was suddenly nervous.

Chapter 3

"Oh, don't keep that old thing. I doubt very much that anyone would ever want to wear that style again." Mac knew that she wouldn't, but someone would. The dress was gorgeous. "You don't dress up much, do you, my dear?"

"Not if I can get away with flip flops and shorts. I'm going to put this in the pile we're going to have Vinnie go through. I think she might be able to sell it." Suzette nodded and smiled at her. The *give to the clothing drive* pile was much smaller than the *Vinnie* pile. "Do you suppose that anyone has touched these things in all the time you've been gone?"

"Doubtful. I do know that our butler has the room aired out on occasion. I'm not sure why…perhaps he expects us to return to a fresh room someday." Mac liked this woman and her husband. They were funny and took their deaths like it was something they had accepted. There were times when she thought maybe Hugh had been adopted, but when she saw father and son together, she could see some of the mannerisms Hugh had picked up from his father. "Do you think you can, for me, put a slice of lemon in that tea and hum at how delicious it is? I've not had a good cup of tea in…well, a very long time."

"I can do that. But I'm stopping at cream in it. If I wanted a glass of milk, there had better be cookies on a tray for me too." They both laughed as Mac put the slice of lemon in the tea. She wasn't a big fan of having her tea this way, but the woman had been so very nice to her since they'd started this project of going through her clothing. "Why didn't Hugh hire someone to come and take care of this for him? Or have the staff do it? There seems to be plenty of them around."

"I don't know. I suppose, like the butler, he expects us to come through the door and demand that our rooms be put to rights as they had been. I don't think that he's dealt well with all of this. And when he was in the hospital for so long, Hugh, his father, and I were just trying to deal with our own deaths, and we didn't think that it was unhealthy for our home to be as it was before. Several times we thought for sure he was going to join us, but he hung on. I think he regrets that, don't you?" Mac knew that Hugh was depressed a great deal, and she thought he might have been a little too close to the edge at times, but she had no idea if he wished he'd died the day they had. "That man that shot us, he worked for us, did you know that?"

"Yes, but only since we've gotten here. I think that Drew knew the story, but not all of it, and I had no idea until we got here that Hugh even had a castle here." His mother nodded and walked over to the jewelry box that looked as big as her refrigerator at home. Suzette had asked to have it opened so she could look at the things there, but she had yet to comment on any of them.

"We sent him to boarding school when he was younger.

It was the thing to do, I suppose, but he did learn a great deal from it. But I missed him so very much. When he'd come home on vacations we'd go do so many things with him. A few times we even met him in the States and wandered around there to see all the places he was reading about." Suzette sounded so sad that Mac thought she should change the subject. As she continued, she realized that she was trying to tell her something important. "When we asked him to come by the office that day, it was...it was a game that we played with him. Or at least his father did. It was to show him who was in charge. We both knew then that it was our son most of the time, but my love wanted to bring him in line, as he called it, and that day had been no different. We have regretted that since."

Mac told her that she doubted that he saw it. Then what she was saying hit her. "You think you brought him to the building to be hurt? Not possible, Suzette. From what I've heard, the man was set on killing your entire family, as well as your household when he was done there. He would have, I'm sure, gotten to Hugh sooner or later if he'd not already been there, but there he had a chance to survive, I think, because the people there helped until an ambulance arrived. Also, the police were on their way, and by him calling them when he did, he also saved a lot of people. It's a shame the man was killed without giving good reason why, but he's gone and you had nothing to do with it."

"But we could have done something to save him, couldn't we?" Mac asked her what she could have done differently. "We could have had better security. The technology was there. Not like it is now, but we could have, so when Mr. Dunn, the man that killed us, was fired, we could have taken care that his badge no longer worked. I was sure we had, but he got in because we were lax on that. I worked with him, the young man. I had no idea that he was capable of such a thing. I don't think anyone did."

"Yeah, and I could have had a motorized kayak had I known some asshole was going to try and toss me over the edge of the falls a few months back. But I didn't, and I got hurt. You can't always be ready for everything." Mac snorted. "Hindsight is always perfect. You did what you did, and there isn't shit you can do about it now. Thinking of all the things you should have done or wish you would have done will not bring you back, nor will it change the outcome of that day. Done is done, as my dad used to say to me."

"Did he also mention that you were somewhat rude?" Mac nodded and told her all the time. "I don't believe you listened to him overly much. Or he should have disciplined you more, perhaps.... But I must say, you are a breath of fresh air. And I do like you. A great deal. I'm sure your dad was very proud of you too."

"Thanks, you're not so bad yourself. And he was. Very much so. My dad was my world. Now Drew and the kids are."

As they sorted through the rest of the first closet, Suzette told her about the day she'd been murdered. It was as if she needed someone to talk to about it that hadn't been there. Someone that she could bounce things off of.

"Burton was a good man when he wanted to be, though strange at times too. However, that day, he came into the offices like he had not a care in the world about what he was doing. I was in my office working on some things for the village when I heard the first of the gunshots and screaming. When Hugh called me, I knew that he had to be safe, so I told him to get away and save himself. Then my door opened and Burton killed me, telling me that he'd already killed my husband beforehand. I was surprised that he'd been able to get to me. Burton had been fired, and his badge shouldn't have allowed him to get to my floor. But there he was. He was sad though. Burton was never one to hide how he was feeling, and it was usually just to complain about anything and everything." She made her way back to the jewelry again before continuing. "There wasn't even time for me to say a word before he spoke, then he pulled out his gun and shot me in the chest. Just like that. As if I wasn't a person he'd just worked with for several years. I fell back, disbelieving that he had shot me, and that was when he stood over me and told me he was going to wipe out my entire family, and then my house too. I had to die, he told me. It was only fair that I be dead as well. Then the bullet hit me in the head."

"Did you ever find out why he thought you all had to die?" Suzette said that she had not. "Even later, there was no reason that you could think of? I'm sure that you and your husband talked about it."

"Oh yes, he did speak to us when he'd been killed by the police a few days later. We were grieving, you see, so I'm never sure that I got it right, and asking Hugh wasn't helpful at all since he'd been killed too, you see...the shot to the head was the last one he received, and it ended his life. The scar on his cheek, they think that was a gunshot too, but Hugh told me that he'd fallen against the armor in his office and got cut that way. Then the leg shot. I was never clear on why he shot us that way. But he did say that we had no rights to live when we'd killed her. And that we had to pay." Mac cleared her throat. "Oh yes. The reason. He said that we destroyed his family. But to be honest with you, Mac, as far as I knew, he had no one but his parents. His mother and father were very nice people, but healthy and happy so far as that went. I know that they're gone. I know that we were in touch with them off and on over the years before this. But as far as his family being destroyed, I have no idea why he'd blame that on us. They both died after Hugh and I did."

"Was there anyone else?" She said that she didn't think so, but wasn't really sure. "I can have someone look for you. Maybe there was someone that he knew, a cousin or someone that he believes you hurt in some way."

"Maybe, but I wouldn't know who it might have been. We tried our best to make sure that everyone had what they needed. Even going so far as to set up a fund that would...." When she paused, Mac knew that she had remembered something. "He had a sister. I don't remember her name, but she was a little bitty thing and would occasionally come to the house with Burton when he brought apples, or other fruit, to the cook. She was ill. Very ill, and couldn't be out long or she'd end up in the hospital for one thing or another. Her immune system was very weak, and she'd get anything that was going around. But unlike other children, she wouldn't recover quickly. I know that for a long time we had fundraisers to try and help them raise enough money to get the proper care for her. You don't suppose he blames that on us, do you?"

"Did she die?" Suzette said that she didn't know, but had assumed so. "That could be it. She might have succumbed to whatever had made her sick, and that was why he blamed you." Suzette asked her if she could find out. "I think so. Do you know anything about her? Or maybe what hospital it was?"

"There is only the one. Do you suppose you could figure out if the poor thing passed and what from? I'd like to know for no other reason than I'd like to know if we helped the girl in any way. I know that you said what is done is done, but I'd really like to know what this man thinks we might have done to him that he felt the need to kill us all." Mac said that she'd look for them. "Good. I'm so glad. Now. Let's see you in one of my old dresses. I'd really love to see you all dressed up before we have Vinnie go through them."

The rest of the afternoon went fast. As she began going through the jewelry chest with her, Suzette seemed to get sad. Each piece that was brought out, she not only knew the date it was given to her but by whom as well. Finally Mac told her that she wasn't going to do this.

"I thought you had to take all these things out of the room for him?" Mac just shook her head. "You do know that he won't do it. And as much as I hate going down this lane, I think that it has to be done."

"It will be. When he finds himself a wife. And he will. I just know it." Suzette asked her if she really thought so. "Yes, I do. He's been alone for a long time now. And he's the last of the men to get married. I know that he's meant to find himself someone that will keep him from being sad and lonely all the time. He needs to be happy."

"Oh, that would be so wonderful. I love him so very much, and I hate seeing him this way." Mac did as well. "Drew and you have been so wonderful for him. You know that, don't you? And when he told us we were finally going to get to meet you, I had a feeling that we'd be...well, I didn't think you'd be very receptive of us. Two old dead people just hanging around."

"I think you're amazing. And your husband is funny. But I do think Hugh is going to meet his other half. We just have to figure out who she might be." Suzette asked if she thought it might be Mary. They all had talked about her when Hugh

47

wasn't around, and Mac had wondered about her too. "I don't know. From what you've said about her, she's sort of a bitch, don't you think? Anyway, whoever she is, I'm sure that she'll be wonderful for him. And us too. We'll be one huge family then."

Mac hoped that more than anything, and decided to have Steele look as hard as he could for Mary. And if she was out there, Mac would do everything she could, including but not limited to kidnapping her, to bring the two of them together if she was his other half. And if not, then Mac knew where to hide the bodies. Or Vinnie would. Things would be perfect.

~~~

Peach watched the comings and goings of the household. She had no idea why she liked the family that was housesitting for Mac, but she did. And even though she should have found herself somewhere to winter out weeks ago, she found herself hanging out at the house more and more. But the whole England thing bothered her a great deal.

What could the connection be? She knew there had to be one. Sure it was a big country, but her luck had never been on the side of being good. Mostly it was bad luck or none at all. Her mother had taught her that part. And her father had lived by the rule most of her life; he'd always been looking for the other shoe to drop, and it did most of the time. Her dad hadn't been a pessimist but he had been, as he called himself, a realist. There were two sides to every story and no one was perfect, he used to tell her…that and other sayings that she still had no idea what they meant.

Shifting to her human side, she pulled on her secondhand clothing as she stood in the barn, and watched the men as they worked on the big addition to the house. When they were finished, the house was going to be huge, and she couldn't wait to see it. Peach wondered why she cared, but let that thought drift away. She just did, that's all.

Peach had been in the house before, off and on over the years as Mac had had the upgrades done to it, as well as when she'd been hurt last fall. Peach would go into the yard as her cat and play with the puppy, which had been fun after he figured out that she wasn't going to hurt him. The two of them had romped and played in the yard for hours at a time while they'd been the only ones around. Then Drew had shown up and she began watching over him as well, especially from the woman that had threatened them almost daily. Mrs. Dutch had not been a nice person, and even meaner than any of them had thought.

Several times Peach had snapped the traps that had been set in Mac's yard…whether for the wildlife that came up to the house or the dog, Peach didn't know. But even before the household was up and about, Peach had begun searching the yard for not just traps, but poisoned food as well. Every day she'd found things that were just cruel, and had wanted to confront the stupid woman about them.

Almost as if she'd called to him, the dog came into the barn, the darkest deepest part of it where she hid, and she smiled when he yipped quietly to her. Reaching into her stash of treats for him, she handed him one as she told him what a fine job he'd done of not being loud. She did not want any extra attention right now.

"It's really too bad that you can't let me know what is going on with them. It would certainly make me rest easier if they weren't trying to find me after all this time." A lot of things would make her rest easier, but that was her own doing, not the fact that she was running. "I'm almost tempted to leave now, go up into the mountains and hide out until I'm sure."

Since coming to the States all those years ago she'd been on the run. Being changed into a cat was not something that she would have agreed to, but it had saved her life. Only to have it torn upside down when things happened that were well beyond her control. Her family had been ruined to the point where her father had died. Then when she'd arrived here things hadn't gotten any better, as every American who read knew about the murders of the McGuires, as well as the family who had caused them such grief. Her mother died a few months later from exhaustion, as well as stress. Peach had been on the run since, trying to outrun a past that caught up with her all the time.

"You'd think I would learn to just keep to myself, wouldn't you?" Rory had no answers, and neither did she really. "If I thought you'd stay with me, I'd love to take you with me. But I know that young James loves you, and Becky has grown quite fond of you as well. I should just go. I have more than enough blankets now. There is no reason whatsoever I should stay. I even have enough food and water this time, provided that winter doesn't last longer than normal. And wood, too, for the cold nights."

But she just couldn't make herself leave. There was something keeping her here. And as little as she knew about this family or the one watching the house, Peach felt a connection to them. As she made her way to the loft of the barn and her stash of food and water, she knew that she'd have to make another trip up the mountain again soon. There she had all the comforts of home, except the company. She was going to miss Rory.

"Peach?" Stilling when she heard her nickname, she waited to see who would be coming in the doorway. Fading back into the shadows, Peach tried to even out her breathing as well as her heart rate. She knew that the woman coming for her would be able to hear both without any problems. "It's Kari Bennett. You spoke to my husband earlier. I would like to ask you something."

Coming out of the place where she'd been hiding by moving down the ladder slowly, when she stood solidly on the ground, she looked over at the woman who was also a cat. They were related, she supposed, in that they were both felines, but that was where things ended. The woman was also something of a powerhouse, and Peach was simply a cat who answered to no one.

"I'm here." Kari turned and looked at her, but Peach wasn't fooled by the smile. She really wasn't the trusting sort of person. "I know that you're more than likely pissed about me marking your mate, but I wanted to talk to him, and I figured that was better than me doing so naked."

"Thank you for that, but that's not why I'm here. I wanted to ask you if you wanted to help me out. Not a big deal if you don't, but I have to deal with this shithead in town again, and maybe if you go with me, sort of a force of women, you can keep me from tearing his throat out. Not that he doesn't deserve it, but I think I'd have trouble hiding the body." If it was a joke, Peach didn't understand it. She knew where two bodies were right now. Not that she'd killed either of them, but she'd put them in the deep cavern so that no one would find them. "What do you say?"

"What person is it?" She told her. "That man needs to have his throat ripped out. I'd gladly help you with that part. But I don't see why you need me to go with you. I'm pretty sure that you're more than capable of taking care of several men like him."

51

"Thank you. And I can, but I'd get my ass in more trouble than I can handle right now. I have to be there for my daughter when she gets older. Not that I don't think my husband can raise her, but he'd never let her date, and he'd have to go to prison the first time a boy came by to pick her up." Peach asked her why before she thought about how friendly she was getting with this woman. "He'd kill them. No other reason than he tells me he was a boy once and had the same sort of feelings that he knows they'd have. I'm saving him by not killing that man. And you'd help me do that. By being there as a calming force."

"I see." She really didn't but nodded anyway. "You don't know me; why would you ask me to accompany you on such a thing?"

"I don't know, other than Steele said he liked you, and you didn't kill him when he was talking to you. Aster, his sister, was there too. She's gone now, but she and Steele hang out a great deal. I love her too, but.... Anyway, I'd really like to get to know you."

"I've no reason to help you, nor do you have any reason to get to know me." Kari cocked her head at her, but Peach was more upset that the woman wanted to be her friend than she was focusing on what she was saying to the woman. "I've a great many things to do before I leave, and there is no time for me to—"

"You're not from around here, are you?" Peach took a step back and gauged how far away the exit was. "I'm not going to do anything to you, but I do want to make sure that whoever you're hiding from doesn't come here and hurt my family. And that would include the ones that live here."

"No. No one will come for me here. I swear to you, nobody here knows who I am. And I'm leaving soon, as I have said." Kari nodded, but didn't say anything. But Peach had an overwhelming urge to continue to explain. "Those that are looking for me might not be looking for me anymore. It's been a long time."

"The people that changed you, right?" Peach didn't say anything, letting the other woman think what she wanted. No, she wasn't being hunted by the woman who had changed her. Besides, Peach had a feeling she was dead anyway. "I have the same thing. Changed against my will. Were you kidnapped and forced to endure this, or was it something else?"

"No, it was something else." Kari nodded and said nothing more about it. There really was more to it than that, but for now, that's all Peach was willing to share. "I would very much like for you to not say anything about me. I'm hiding here, yes, but as I said, I'll be moving along soon."

"All right. But Drew and Mac, they're worried about you. Before they left they told us several times to make sure you were safe and not bothered." Peach nodded, too touched by emotion to say anything. "If you could help me out on this, I'd really appreciate it. I might even have you a nice thick steak ready if you want to join us for dinner tonight."

As much as that sounded great, she knew that she'd not be joining them. Peach knew that she was getting too close to them as it was. But she couldn't think of one reason why she shouldn't go with the woman. There were things she could get, small items that weren't available for her anywhere else, so she mentally made herself a list. As she made her way out to the large SUV that had arrived when these people had, she thought of the last time she'd been in a car of any kind.

"Is Peach your real name?" Peach told her it wasn't. Her brother had called her that when she'd been younger she told her, before she could think what a stupid person she'd become in the last ten minutes. "I see. Did he own a peach orchard or something?"

"Or something." Peach expected her to demand and might have told her if she had, but Kari only nodded. "You're not what I expected. I thought you to be demanding and ordering me away. You have that over me. Your power and strength."

"Why would I do that? I mean, this isn't even my house." True, but she was sort of bossy and said that to her. "Yeah, I get that a lot. I am bossy. Overbearing as well, if you want to know the truth. But I'm loveable too."

Peach couldn't help it, she laughed. The woman was certainly certifiable, but she was nice as well. As they made their way into town toward the hardware store to meet up with the man who had given Kari trouble earlier, Kari did most of the talking. Peach just listened, as she was pretty sure she wasn't required to answer anyway.

Pulling up in front of the place, Kari looked at her. "Hugh and the rest of our friends are coming back in a few days. I'd very much like to have a big dinner to celebrate. Having you there would mean a great deal to Drew and Mac…as I said, they're worried about you and your safety." Peach asked her why they'd care. "You have become important to them. And to us. Steele said you talked to him today. That's going to make them feel pretty good about things as well when they call the next time."

"I'm leaving soon. I should have been gone long before now. I have to get out of here before winter sets in." Peach was thinking that she sounded a great deal like a broken record, and tried to think of something else to say. But Kari asked her why. "I have my reasons."

"I'm sure, but I would like for you to think about it. As I

said, it would mean a great deal to Drew and Mac." She got out of the vehicle then and Peach watched her. As she waited for her on the sidewalk, Peach thought of all the reasons why this woman would not want her around. Then she realized the name of the person she said was coming back. Hugh, she'd said Hugh was coming back.

She felt cold, then hot. Her cat started to hum along her body until she was sure she was going to take her. The next thing she knew, the door was open and her head was between her knees.

"Breathe. Just in and out. Breathe for me." She could hear Kari's voice, but the words were sort of jumbled. "Come on, hold her for me or we're going to be in big shit here. Just hold on and breathe for us."

Peach did too, forcing air out of her tight chest to have to work twice as hard to bring it back in. She knew she stayed like that for several minutes, her head down with Kari telling her to breathe, but it wasn't until she sat up and looked at the woman that she spoke a name she'd not said or heard others say in years.

"Hugh McGuire, is that the Hugh that's coming here soon?" Kari nodded. "Lord Whimmpington the tenth, Earl of the McGuire castle?"

"Castle? I have no idea, but for the sake of argument, let's say you're right. What is it about him that nearly had your cat coming and you scaring the shit out of me?" Why indeed, her mind screamed at her. "Peach, you have to tell me what's going on, or I'm going to have to do some very not so nice things to get some answers."

Pushing her way out of the car, she moved to the sidewalk. It was time to move. Not just out of the town, but even the mountain wasn't going to be a place she'd feel safe right now.

As she entered the hardware store, Peach thought of the list of last minute things she was going to need, then as soon as they were back to the barn, she was going to be out of there. Even the thought of hanging around to see the young man again was something she knew she couldn't do. Time was running out. Hugh was alive and he was going to know she was here.

"If you think you're going to get away before I get some answers, you're crazier than I am." Peach said nothing. There was nothing holding her back now, other than the blooming friendship she had here. "I mean it. I'm going to get what I want."

"I'm sorry to disappoint you, Kari, but you might want to get used to it. As I have said too many times to count, I have to go. Now more than ever."

Kari started to speak again, but the man who owned the store came from his domain in the back. His next words should have warned her that nothing was going to be easy about this.

"Well, if it's not the woman who thinks she knows more than me when it comes to pricing my shit. I thought I told you not to come back here. I have no use for your kind in my store." Then he looked over at Peach and laughed. "What the fuck did you do, go out and find yourself another female to try and show off? Everyone knows that women only have two places in this world. One of them is on their back, the second is on their knees. Where you should be about now."

His laugh had Peach turning, and in that minute all her anger came at her and she let her cat take her.

Chapter 4

Hugh had thought to wait in the car, because he was tired from the long trip and just wanted to go home, but it was hot and stuffy, and they were taking a good deal longer to get things settled in the police station than he thought they would. Getting out, he drew in a deep breath and could smell the country air even as he made his way to the jail. Kari and another woman had been arrested earlier this morning, and now Steele was there with Drew and Mac, trying to get them out. He had no idea what had happened, but since they'd come back a couple days earlier than expected, Steele had asked for help and they'd driven straight here from the airport.

The castle was now his. Not only that, but the village had decided he could marry when he wanted, provided he helped them put in a new public school, as well as doing some upgrades on the library. Things he was sure had more to do with the ghosts whispering in their ears than the real need for him to fulfill his part of the will his parents had set up for him. Agreeing to the terms they had ready for him, Hugh was feeling pretty good until Sander came to him and told him what it was going to cost him to do this. Not in monetary funds, but simply that he had to be there more than he was. They wanted a full time benefactor, not someone who popped in on occasion.

"Your friend went to talk to them yesterday on your behalf. I don't believe they had anything to do with you having to be on the property all the time. But it's a good solid plan if you ask me." He asked him which friends. "Mr. Mullins and his lovely wife. Also, I do believe that there were some others there, but I can't be certain about them. I can't see them as you can, but I overheard some of the others talking about them."

"Ghosts, you mean." Sander had only shrugged. "And what is it they said to them that got them to agree to just about turn over the city keys to me? I'm sure there was more than just the thought of getting a new building put in, as well as some upgrades on a couple more."

"I do believe...." Hugh had just growled low at him. "All right, sir. I heard that your mother whispered in their ears. Telling them that if you were to leave here and take all your funding with you, the town would fall into such disrepair that no one would live there. And wouldn't a nice new grade school be so much better than no people in the town at all?"

"I couldn't have taken all the money, Sander. And I'm pretty sure that my mother knows that. I have to have the house maintained so long as I live." Again Sander just shrugged. "You know how much I hate that, don't you?"

"Yes, I do, and I think that I'm enjoying this." He grinned at him, and Hugh hadn't been able to help it, he grinned back. "You are able to find you a bride of your choosing, sir, and fall in love. Shouldn't that be enough?"

"I'm not going to do that, and we both know it. First of

all, who the hell would love me? And secondly, I don't have any room in my heart for love. Besides the fact that I have too much baggage to bring someone else into my life right now. And I don't know how to love anyone." Sander had said nothing, though he might well have said a lot. His look said a great deal. "I know that you're looking for Mary. Billy and Carlton aren't very good at keeping secrets, if you must know. Leave her alone. And for Christ's sake, please don't play matchmaker for me. She's...if you had asked, I could have told you where she is and what she's been doing. But trust me, Sander, she is not going to ever be my wife. The woman is a shark, and not likely to make the townspeople any happier than she would me."

"I don't think they wanted her to be your wife so much as someone you could talk to. An old friend, I guess. I think that she's been found in the States, believe it or not. I wish that I could be there for the happy reunion, but my wife and I leave in the morning for Cairo. What a lovely time we'll have too. I cannot thank you enough for this." Hugh just waved him off and asked him what they'd found out about Mary. Hugh was sure that they hadn't even scratched the surface of Mary Manchester. "The girl is not married, nor has she ever been. There are no children, and as far as we can ascertain, there never were any. Her mother visits her on occasion; her father is much too busy to come with her, but they do talk. I'm to understand that they're giving her money. However, I don't know how much nor where the money goes once it leaves here. And I'm not quite sure where the funds are coming from. I am looking into that as we speak. Mary has a nice little apartment in the city that she barely keeps up. I think she's been moving around a great deal trying to find her feet in the world, and has settled finally."

"Can you stop this…this man hunt to find me a wife or a fuck buddy?" Sander said he didn't think there was anyone who could stop Mrs. Bennett when she had her mind set. "You might be right about that. But I don't want to see her. I doubt very much she wants me to see her either."

"I don't know, Hugh. I've never spoken to her, but there have been others that have. Mrs. Bennett seems to think that Miss Mary will be glad to see you, and I don't have any knowledge as to why she'd not want to." Hugh didn't answer his unspoken question. "Hugh, she's fallen on some hard times since she moved. I think perhaps that she's not been very successful with her money and has invested poorly, if at all."

And now, in just one more day, he was about to meet the woman he'd had more sex with against trees than anyone he'd ever met. She was coming to the house tomorrow, Drew had told him, and he'd better be on his best behavior. Smiling, Hugh made his way into the courthouse, where the jail as well as the mayor's offices were, and sat in the chair to wait. It wasn't much cooler in here, but it was a good deal more entertaining.

Drunks were a way of life in any small or large town, and it looked like this town, the one that he'd recently bought a house in that bordered the property that Drew and Mac owned, had a few that were as colorful as they were loud. This man was yelling about how his wife, his dead wife, had told him to drink the liquor that he'd stolen so that there would be no evidence that he'd stolen it when they came to arrest him.

"I did no such thing. All I said to him was that if he drank it all, the police wouldn't need the empty bottles to know that he'd robbed the liquor store…they'd find his dead stinking body in a pool of his nasty urine to know." She looked over at him when he laughed. "You can see me? You really can see me?"

Hugh nodded and looked around the room to sort of tell her that he couldn't talk to her. She must have gotten it because she came to sit by him and told him that he didn't have to look at her when he spoke. She'd just ask him yes or no questions.

"Are you with them Justice Boys? And if you are, can you help me out?" He nodded to both questions. "I'm sick of watching this man kill himself faster every day, and I want you to send me over. Can you do that? Or if not, know someone that can?"

Shaking his head no, he did nod to the man coming out of the back room. When she asked him if that was Mr. Bennett, her question was answered by the officer at the front desk calling out his name to say he was leaving with his wife and to have access to the front door. Like they all should run for cover now that Kari was out of the cell and free to hurt them. Which didn't look like the case to him.

"I see, and he can do it, Mr. Bennett. I know he can, but will he?" Again he nodded and leaned back on the chair. "You're worried about the old fart, aren't you? I am as well, but I just can't follow him around trying to keep him out of trouble any more. To be honest with you, I hated doing it when I was alive. Now…well, I've had enough, and he's not going to listen to me now any more than he did when I was harping on his ass all the time before."

Hugh wasn't worried about the man, and thought perhaps that the wife harping on him all the time, as she said, was what had him drinking. Hugh wondered if their relationship had ever changed since the woman died, or had it gotten worse? Some people were better off not seeing who was hanging around them all the time. And this man appeared to be one of them.

As Steele came out of the room with a smiling Kari, he was carrying little Aster. Hugh wondered about the other woman when no one else appeared, but said nothing. He'd heard there were two, and when he stood up, he noticed that Kari was laughing hard enough that she had to lean on her husband.

"We have to go to the back lot to pick up Kari's pet. It's a small wonder that they didn't put her down when this started. I guess the man in the hardware store is saying that a woman—a bitch, I think he called her—had come in and just turned into a cat. Kari thinks he was drunk." Hugh started to ask what pet when Steele winked at him and continued in a much lower voice. "She's a shifter, leopard, and lost it when the man they were set to see got pissy with them. It's the one that has been at Mac and Drew's place. Remember?"

"To be fair, it was my fault. I should have known she was too much on edge to help me deal with his ass." Kari kissed him on the cheek as she told him the rest of the story. "When he started spewing things that were just a little on the shitty side, she lost her cat. It was a beautiful sight to behold, but also a little dangerous. Had I not thought to tell them the cat belonged to Mac...well, I'm pretty sure that they would have shot her when she stood there snarling and snapping at them. By the way, I think she knows you."

"Me?" Kari nodded and took the little girl from Steele while he paid the fines. "I don't know anyone around here other than the people who work for Mac and Drew."

"She nearly turned as white as a sheet when I mentioned you were coming home. And so you know, her name is Peach. She asked me if you were titled. I don't remember now what

it was. Something about the tenth of some Winnipeg place."
The name, a nickname, triggered a long ago memory, but that
was all it was, a tug. He knew the name, or at least thought he
had, but didn't really know for sure. "Whimmpington. That's
it. And she mentioned that you have a castle. Do you? And do
you know her?"

"Not that I know of, but there was a neighbor that had a
lot of people working for him. Her father owned the orchard
where we lived when I was growing up, but he worked at
the newspaper in town. Sort of as an all-around kind of guy.
His daughter and I had...we had some fun out there. Her dad,
I think, called her something other than Mary, but I'm not
sure it was Peach." Hugh completely ignored the reference
to his name or the castle, hoping that they could discuss it
another time. Kari asked him if it was Mary Manchester. "Yes.
I was going to talk to you about her anyway. I don't want
her coming around me. She was a nice enough person back
when we were kids and I needed to get laid, but things have
changed, Kari, and so have I. I have enough shit going on, and
I don't want to have to deal with her too."

"I didn't do anything, but I think it's sweet that you think
so. As for shit in your life? Deal with it. I know nothing about
either of you other than someone was looking for her, this
Peach person, and that she was starting to come around until
you were mentioned. As for Mary whatever, I don't care
about her either, and had shit to do with finding her. Whether
or not you two hook up again, it's none of my business. And
if this Peach girl is Mary, it might be a moot point anyway, as
I think she's planning to run as soon as we get to the house. I
have to take her home now and see if I can help her."

Hugh tried to think if Mary had been converted to a cat.
He didn't think so, but he'd sort of lost track of her once or

twice over the ensuing years. It was possible, he supposed, but unlikely. She wouldn't have done something like that and kept it from her parents. And he was sure they didn't know about it.

The big cat got into the back of the car with Kari. There was nothing for her to put on, so it was either stay a cat or be naked. Hugh was so furious right now that he didn't care if the lot of them walked back to the house naked. He rode back to Mac and Drew's house with Steele.

Neither man said anything during the drive. He wasn't sure, but he thought perhaps Steele was laughing at him. He didn't care what he was doing, but Hugh was plotting and planning. There was nothing holding him here any longer, and he was going back to his home country. The hell with all of them.

As soon as he was in the drive, he went into the house to gather his things up and to call for a plane to be ready for him. The sooner the better. But as soon as he walked in the door, he nearly fell back. There she was. Mary Manchester. And she looked about as cold and calculating as he remembered her being. And the years, it seemed, had been very unkind to the woman.

~~~

When Peach came down the stairs from dressing in the clothing that Kari gave her, she watched the couple in front of her. She knew them both. Mary's parents had been in charge of the trees, and Peach's parents had worked for them. Peach started to turn and leave, but Mary saw her before she could make good on her need to be gone.

"Well, look who it is. Kimber Dunn, the one person in the world I thought I'd never see again. Christ, I had hoped you were dead." Peach said nothing, but glanced at Hugh.

She was sure he wouldn't remember her, and when he said her name, she took a step back to hold onto the stair railing. "Yeah, that's who it is, Kimber Dunn, sister of the man who murdered your entire family. Hugh, whoever brought her here is cruel, don't you think? Beyond cruel to do this to us."

"Peach?" Kimber nodded, then shook her head at Kari. "Are you Kimber or Peach? And what does she mean that you're the sister of.... Your brother was Burton Dunn?"

"Yes, I'm her. Both actually. Peach is my nickname. My brother gave me that name when he said that I was his little—" Mary cut her off with a harsh, unfriendly laugh. "I should go. I have to go."

"I don't think so. Not until everyone knows you for what you really are." Her cat hummed along her body, and Mary laughed again. "You're not even a human being any more, are you? Christ, this just gets better all the time. Kimber Dunn is an animal. And you're here to what? Hook up with Hugh? I don't think so. He's all mine, honey, and will be long after you're gone."

"Shut the fuck up, Mary." Everyone turned to Drew when he spoke. "This is my house, and I will not have you treating guests of mine like this. Hugh, take that woman to the living room and stifle her. Mac, can you see to Kimber...Peach...what is it you want to be called?"

"Kimber. My name is Kimber. But I'd like to go now, if you don't mind."

But before she could tell them thanks for everything, Kari and Mac took her to the right of the stairs and to the kitchen area and sat her in a chair. Kimber sat there when they said nothing, and thought it was time she explained a few things. But knowing where to start was hard.

"I didn't know what was going to happen that day. I had

no idea that my brother was going to do any of those things he was accused of."

"I should hope not." A glass of water was set in front of her, and she only stared at it as Mac continued. "We thought you were the same person…Mary and Peach, I thought that you were her. I'm glad you're not. Christ, that woman is a piece of work, and I only just met her when we swung by her house to get her. Did you know that she demanded that we take her by a parlor to have her hair done before we brought her here? What for, I asked her, and she said that she was going to marry Hugh and wanted to make a good impression."

Hugh walked in the room and she stood up. Kimber braced herself for the slap or whatever he was going to do to her. Whatever it was, she knew that it wouldn't be a tenth of what she deserved though. He asked Mac and Kari to give him a minute. When they left, he sat down and let out a long breath.

His scent hit her. Not just his breath blowing over her, but the scent that was uniquely his. Her cat rolled against her skin, making herself known to both the man and her. But instead of backing away from her, Hugh reached out and ran his fingers down the length of her arm over the fur that moved along her skin there.

"Don't." He didn't listen to her plea, but moved his hand down to her fingers when she tried to pull away from him. When he lifted one up, Kimber could see her nails, or those of the cat, and pulled her hand from his. He stared at her for several seconds before he put his hands in his lap. "I don't know what to say to you, or her. For some reason, Mary has always disliked me and I was never sure why."

"You're his sister, Burton's sister?" She nodded, her cat begging her now to touch the man in front of her. "I didn't remember you until I saw you. Peach…Burton called you his peach. I thought you were gone. Dead. I thought you had died. I guess you didn't."

He was babbling. She was too, but it was kind of cute on him. Hugh had always had a way about him that would make you believe every word that came from his mouth. If he said it was cold and the temperature was over a hundred, you'd have to believe him.

"No, I didn't die. I was sick but…. I read about what Burton did. When I was…when we…. Why are you here?" Mate, her mind screamed at her. Mate. Take him. But instead of heeding what she knew would never happen, she stood up and so did he. "I didn't know what he was going to do. I wasn't even aware that he'd come by to see me, but Mary had been there, with her mother. My mom told me when I woke up. I…my mom had gone out, and they were just there when she came back, she said. I had no idea what he was about to do or I would have said something. I'm not sure what, but I would have helped if I could have."

"Do you know what he was pissed about?" She did know, at least she'd found out later. For some reason he blamed Hugh's parents for what had happened to her. But she said nothing to him. Her body was having a hard enough time just staying away from him. And dealing with this wasn't going to help. "Are you okay?"

"I have to go." Before she could make her way to the door, Kari came back in. And she looked at Hugh, then at her again. "I'm going to go now. I wanted to thank you for bailing me out. I'd like to say that I'll pay you back, but I don't have any money, and nothing that you'd find very—"

"Is he your mate, Kimber? Is that why I can hear your cat calling to him?" She shook her head…there was no way this was going to happen to her. Not with this man. "Kimber, you do know that there is nothing you can do about this. If he's your mate, you're as good as together now."

"What do you mean, mate? I'm not sure where you're getting your information, Kari, but that can't be true. I don't want to be anyone's mate. Now or ever." Kimber felt as if he'd slapped her. And in a way, she wished that he had. She was sure that the pain would have been less. "Kimber? What is she saying? You think I'm going to be your mate? Talk to me, please. Tell Kari that she's mistaken, and that you're nothing to me."

She shoved by him. Her heart shattered on the floor at his feet. Even as she tore the door from its hinges, the broken wood falling in her wake, she moved out of the house and let the cat take her. When someone said her name, she moved, leaping over the deck railing and down to the riverbed to follow it to where she knew at least some safety was.

It took her an hour to move up to the caves she'd been staying in for some time now. Backtracking when she could, going upstream when the water was calm enough to let her swim up it as her cat, she covered her tracks as best she could. The caves had been her saving grace, and now it was over too.

Wintering there for the last several years, she'd come to think of the place as her home. It was where she could simply hide out when all the other residents went into their other homes after summer was over. Most all of them anyway, except Mac. She could come and go as she pleased up here and no one was the wiser. It had been the best place she'd ever found, and the quietest. Now Kimber knew she was going to have to move on.

Shifting to her other self, Kimber pulled on clothing and shoes, then started to gather up what she could take. Water bottles would have to stay…they were too heavy to carry as human or cat. The other things she'd accumulated, such as blankets and extra canned food, would be all right so long as she didn't try to take them all. Matches were shoved in her pack along with a first aid kit she'd never used, as well as her clothing.

When she felt the man, Steele, touch her mind, she blocked him and continued with her work. It wasn't until she was nearly ready to take off that she felt someone in the room with her. Turning slowly, she really wasn't surprised to see Kari and another woman at the mouth of the cave, standing there as if waiting.

"This is my good friend, Vinnie. She is a vampire." The woman nodded, but didn't enter her cave. "She needs for you to invite her in. I guess you've made this your home, and she can't come in until you invite her, and so you know, even not having her come in, she's not going to let you get by her."

"She can try if she wants. Is there a way to keep you out too?" No answer, but a smile that told her to try and there would be hell to pay. "I didn't have anything to do with that man down there, and I had nothing to do with my brother killing his parents. I haven't had any contact with any of them."

"Mary seems to think that you came here just to take him from her. Though why she'd think that is beyond me. She's not a very nice person. Hugh and she have a history, as I'm sure you're aware of, but he's moved on while I don't think she has." Kimber snorted. Everyone had known that they were fuck buddies. Mary told every person she saw. And one day, she swore, he was going to forget to use a condom and then it would all be hers. "You know her too, I'm assuming."

"I do. She can have him. I'm pretty sure that's what they

both want anyway. I have no use for a mate any more than he does." She tried to think around the pain in her heart again. There was no way that there should be anything with only seeing the man the one time, but her cat thought differently. "What are you doing here, anyway?"

"I've come to see you. Bring you back to the house if I can. And to see why you ran. Not really much. And some of it, I think I might know the answers to already." Kimber told her good for her. "By the way, good job on coming here. I had to go back three times over your path to figure out that you were better at this than I was. I had to have a couple of my friends come and find you, then have Vinnie help me."

"I've been running for a long time." Kari asked her why. "I don't have to explain myself to you or anyone. And as for Hugh, I'm betting you know exactly why I ran. He no more wants me in his life than I do him."

"You told me once that you were changed without your knowledge. Did Hugh's parents have anything to do with that? Or is that just something that Burton thought?" Kimber just stared at her. That was something else she'd gotten good at, not talking when people thought she should have. "I can find out, you know. I can just ask Hugh's parents. They're here, by the way. With us."

Kimber felt her heart stop beating. If anyone had said to her before this that when you hurt badly enough, your heart simply gives up, she would never have believed them. But there it was, an empty shell more than it had been before.

"I had nothing to do with their deaths." Kari nodded and looked to her left. So did Kimber. There was nothing there that she could see, but she knew that Kari did. A person could not be a paranormal and not have heard of the things this woman — or any of them, for that matter — could do.

70

"Suzette wants to know how it happened. How you were changed into a cat." Kimber said nothing. It was no one's business, as far as she was concerned. "She asks that you tell her so that she doesn't feel like it's her fault that you're a cat."

"Her fault? How the fuck does she think...? You know what, I don't care. You want to know? Fine." She put down her pack and lifted her shirt up so the scar that had never disappeared after she was made was visible. "The nurse that came in three times a day told me that she was going to help me. I knew I was dying. As close to death as I'd ever been. My kidneys were gone, and I could no longer lift my hands up to even feed myself...not that it mattered. I couldn't hold anything down anyway. Then she came into my room, stripped down, and shifted, right there in front of me. But I was too weak to fight her, and when she jumped up on the bed and bit me, I knew that I'd never survive. Really, I wish that I hadn't."

"She saved your life." Kimber pulled her shirt down and said nothing. "But I can see where you don't think so. And when your brother found out, he decided to kill the McGuires because they provided you with the nurse. Is that right?"

"I really don't know how he found out. Other than the fact that he was there the morning after it happened, I know nothing about what he knew or didn't know. Mary could have told him, I guess. Her version, I'm sure, would have been far from the truth, and how she might have been the one to have thought of it. She was good at that, taking credit for things she had nothing to do with. Though how she knew, I don't know the answer to that either. He'd been nursing his wounds after being fired, Mom said, and asked if he could stay with us a few days. I, of course, was all for that, Burton was my hero back then." Kari nodded and watched the people that Kimber couldn't see. "Burton never could hold down a job, and no one blamed them for firing him. He was an idiot. A wonderful brother, but an idiot all the same."

"Hugh, Lord Hugh, said that they'd worked with him for several months to get his act together. But Burton just couldn't seem to concentrate very long on a single task without getting side tracked. They even got him professional help, but it didn't matter." Kimber knew this, and had heard plenty of times from Burton how nice the McGuires were to him. That was one of the reasons she'd never understood why he'd killed them. "He wants to know why you left the house without speaking to his son, and what your plans are now."

"I'd like to know that as well. Other than the fact that I was a fool." They all turned to Hugh as he filled the doorway. Vinnie was behind him and smiled at her. If she could have, Kimber might have hurt the vampire. As it was, there was nowhere for her to run now that there were several people blocking the doorway. "Kimber, are you really my mate?"

Chapter 5

Vinnie had come to get him. Well, she'd hit him first, then she'd told him off before taking him to the caves. He stretched his jaw again, waiting for an answer from Kimber. He knew that he was going to be sore there for a few days if the pain was any indication. It was no less than he deserved, he supposed. He'd been an ass; more than that, he'd been a selfish prick to Kimber. He watched his parents as they left too, knowing that they were close should something go wrong.

"What are you doing here?" He started to tell her that he'd been brought, but he was pretty sure that wasn't what she meant by the question. "If you'll just have them take you back to the house, I'll be on my way."

"Mary said that you've been waiting here for me. That you'd had this plan to trap me into something. I don't know where she might have come up with that idea, but she also said that you two were friends, that you had confided in her." He had no idea why she thought that was important to him, but Mary had also mentioned that Kimber had had her sights

73

on him for years, and was just jealous of their relationship. Hugh thought the latter was funny as they'd never had one. "Are you friends? The reason I ask is because I didn't think you were. Now or then, as a matter of fact."

"No, I didn't like her when we were younger, and I have no use for her now. She's nothing but a spoiled bitch with a god-like attitude that grates on my last nerve." He started to laugh at her brutal honesty, but didn't. She was seriously pissed off, and he'd already been hit once today. "I think you two are perfect for each other. You should marry her. She's about your type."

"And what type is that?" When she didn't answer him, he smiled. "You're very quiet, aren't you? I remember that as a kid. Your brother would go on and on about this or that, and you'd just sit there saying not a word. Usually you had a book or two with you, but you didn't seem to be a part of even his world."

"You're making that up, or someone told you. You and Burton never hung out together, nor did you ever notice me." But she had him, he'd bet. He wasn't vain, but he knew that she'd hung out with her brother when she'd been able to, just to be where he was. He'd seen her looking at him when she thought no one was watching. "They think he killed your parents because he believed they were responsible for me being like this."

"And what is that?" He had been moving toward her, and when he was close enough to pick up her pack and toss it to the back of the cave, she asked him what he was doing. "I want to talk to you, mostly to apologize to you for my behavior. Seeing Mary like that...well, I knew what she'd been doing since I'd left home. Most of it anyway, but things are coming to light that I wasn't aware of, and I'm making it my business now."

"We don't have anything to talk about, and stop crowding me. I don't like it." He was within touching distance of her now. Close enough that he could smell her, and when he reached out and ran his finger down her cheek, her breathing hitched and her body swayed toward him, for all of a second. "You'll not come to me after being with her, Hugh. Not that I want you, but you reek of her, of sex."

It took his befuddled mind a few seconds to catch up to what she was talking about. And in that few seconds of lapsed concentration she had moved by him and was nearly to the door. Turning quickly, he just managed to grab her arm as she moved out of the cave and into the woods beyond. They both went down in the grassy area, then down the great hill, tumbling ass over head.

Landing at the first flat place, he held her to him. He was hurting, but not like he thought he might have if she hadn't taken some of the hits on the way down. Lifting his head from her shoulder where he was, he looked down at her.

"How come I never noticed what a beauty you were going to be?" She snorted, something that he was sure she did a great deal. "Kimber, what if I told you that I had no idea you were alive, that I thought that whatever had made you so sick had taken your life? But that right now, I can't thank you enough for being here and under me. Why is that? Why do I want you so badly when we don't even know each other?"

"It's all in your head. I told you that you can have Mary, and I know you want her too. That's where you've been." He smiled, and she struggled to get her hand free to no doubt hit him, so he grabbed her hands and held them above her head while she cursed him. Hugh had no doubt that she could pull from him anytime she wanted. But she didn't, and for that he was glad. And there was no way this was only in his head. His need for her was overwhelming. Hugh wanted her as badly as he did his next breath.

"Let me go. My cat will tear you apart."

"No, she won't. She can't hurt me." At least that's what Kari had told him after he'd been helped up from the floor. "She wants me too. And for your information, I was never with Mary today, not for a long time, as a matter of fact. She tried, but there...nothing happened."

Hugh leaned into her throat, a place that he wanted to taste her badly enough that he was willing to risk getting close to her mouth for. When he licked her pounding pulse, he moaned at the heated taste of her. Lifting his head, he looked into her eyes as he rocked into her heat.

"Let me go." Her words said one thing, but her body was telling him something very different. "I mean it, Hugh. Let me up so I can go."

"Are you wet, Kimber? Is your pussy swollen with heat for me?" He could smell her then, and when her legs wrapped around his thighs, he rocked into her over and over. "I would love to take you right now. I know that you'd accept me into your body. Wouldn't you? You'd like for me to fuck you right now. Say it."

"You don't know me. You...do you remember that my brother killed your family?" He buried his nose in her throat again, and this time bit down on the tender skin. "Please don't do this, Hugh. You know as well as I do that you only want someone to fuck, and I'm close for you. Go and find Mary again. I'm sure that...that she can...stop that."

"I have a feeling that fucking you will be more than either of us bargained for." He held her hands in his, but knew that he wasn't so much holding her as he was hanging on. Her fingers had long since curled into his, and he rocked into her again while he lifted her shirt up over her breasts. "I want to suckle your nipples. Taste them as you take your pleasure from me. Will you come? Come hard for me, Kimber?"

When her breasts were exposed to him, he cupped one in his free hand. She was full, and her breast spilled out of his hand as he thumbed her nipple to a hard peak. Taking the large morsel into his mouth, he sucked deeply, feeling her reaction all the way to his toes. When he opened his mouth wider, taking as much of her heavy flesh into his mouth as he could, her hands pulled free of his and she curled her fingers into his hair and held him to her. Christ, he thought, she was going to make him come now. Fully dressed. While in the woods.

Reaching between them, he slid his hand between her legs and pressed hard against the dampness of her pants. That was all it took to bring her. The climax had him pressing against her again and again as she came twice more for him. She had needed him, apparently, as badly as he did her.

She screamed out her releases, and watching her face as she did so, Hugh thought perhaps he'd never seen anything quite so beautiful in his life. When she rocked upward, seemingly begging him for more, he rolled to his back, taking her with him.

"I need to be inside of you. I want to bury my cock deep inside of you while you come like that again." She tore his shirt open, then leaned down and took a nipple into her mouth. When she bit down hard enough for him to feel a pleasurable pain, he held her to him as he jerked at his pants under her. When she sat up again, he watched her pull her blouse up and over her head along with her bra. Hugh sat up and held both of her lovely breasts in his hands while he feasted on the tips. But it wasn't enough. Not for either of them, it seemed. Hugh needed her. Not just her body, he figured out, but her too. All of her.

When she stood up, her breasts still wet from his mouth, Hugh nearly hurt himself pulling his pants open and freeing himself. As he held himself in his hand, pain, the need to come hurting him, he looked up at her when she paused in taking her pants off. There was a large scar on her belly, but other than that, he thought her to be perfect. The most beautiful creature he'd ever seen.

"If we do this, if you fuck me, it'll be too late to turn back. I'll be your mate for all time. Nothing will be able to sever that but death." Her hands didn't move...she was giving him an out, for whatever reason. "Hugh, are you listening to me? Are you understanding what I'm saying?"

"Yes, I understand you, but I'm afraid it's already too late, Kimber." He moved his hands to her pants, pushing her hands away so his could replace them. Watching her, he pulled them off her, slowly moving them down her legs. "I think it's been too late for us to change our minds since the day that our families came together in tragedy."

Pulling her naked body to him, he cupped her ass and brought her to his mouth. Cream made her curls damp for him; her taste, he knew, was going to be better than anything he'd ever had. As he licked her from gate to clit, Hugh suckled her into his mouth and felt her legs tremble. As much as he wanted to drink deeply of her, he knew that he needed to be inside of her. Needed to come deep inside of her as he'd never done with a woman before. Pulling her down to him, laying her on the ground next to him, he shed his pants and rolled his body over hers until he was between her thighs. He wanted to take her then, move his cock at her entrance and take her hard. But she stopped him by jerking his head back before he kissed her.

"I've never had sex before." His mind went into overdrive at her words. "Men just...I've been hiding for so long that I've never had the urge. I didn't want you to think that...you know, that I didn't want this for some reason if I hurt."

A virgin. She was his, and a virgin too. Hugh tried to think what he should do, how to proceed with this, because there was no way they were stopping. Short of her telling him to stop, he was going to make love to this woman, if she let him.

"I'm glad you told me. And I know you want me as much as I do you, love. I'll be gentle, if I can." He reached down and pulled her leg up and curled it over his hip to show her what he wanted her to do. When her other leg lifted up and she wrapped around him, he felt his cock stretch as he felt her heat. "I don't want to hurt you, love, but I will."

Slamming forward without warning her seemed the best way to take her. It might have been painful for her, but he knew that she'd tense up more if he tried to explain to her that she needed to relax. As she held him to her, her legs and arms wrapped tightly around him, he lifted his head and felt his heart twist when he saw her tears. Wiping at them, he told her how incredibly sorry he was.

"It's all right." It wasn't and he told her so. "It really is. I knew that someday someone would...please move or something. I feel like I'm on the edge of something huge, and you're keeping it all to yourself."

Laughter spilled from his mouth, and he complied. He wasn't sure who moaned the loudest when he did, but Christ, she felt wonderful to him. As he moved slowly inside of her, taking his time mostly to keep himself from plowing her, he watched her face for any sign that he was hurting her again.

But he should have known she wasn't going to put up with that. Kimber had never struck him as a person who waited on others to do things for her.

As she dug her fingers into his back, scratching him with her nails, he felt her sheath pull and tighten around him. When she came, screaming loud enough to startle birds from the trees, he felt the power of her climax roll over him, taking him with her. And when she yanked his head to her, his throat exposed to her mouth, he cried out his second release when she bit down hard enough to bring stars to his eyes. He knew what she had done, marked him for others to see.

His cock filled again, his balls tightening to his body as she drank from his vein. Holding her tighter against him, fucking her again as hard as he could, her body bowed up from the ground as she climaxed twice more. Hugh knew the moment that he released inside of her again that they had tightened the bond between them. And when she told him to bite her, to draw blood and drink from her, he knew that nothing, not either of them, would be the same again.

His mouth seemed to have a desire of its own. Even as he tore at her throat, tasting her blood as she came with him again, Hugh knew the real meaning of connection. It was as if they had known each other their entire lives, and that this day, this moment, had been preordained.

The taste of her blood, hot, rich, and full of some spice that he found he loved, made him cross-eyed with his next climax. Even as his body dropped down on hers, exhaustion taking him under, Hugh knew that he had found someone to love him, despite his inability to love her back.

~~~

The sounds of the forest were coming back as she lay on top of him. At some point he'd rolled over, taking her with him, and Kimber hadn't had the energy to move when she could have. Instead, she had rested her head on his heart and listened to it slow, then settle into a normal rhythm. Kimber then watched everyone come to life as the sun went down.

The deer were out now as they were no longer screaming and making noises, and the stag knew that he could safely bring out his herd. Insects and other small creatures came out, scurrying around trying to gather food before the larger animals feasted upon them. As the chain of them grew, so did the noises that they made. Birds screeched in the skies above them, wolves and coyotes began their hunts as well. The sounds of warning were heeded as they moved along the bushes and small trees, looking for anything that would fill their bellies on this night.

Kimber knew just when Hugh woke up, and laid there waiting for him to start telling her why he couldn't be her mate or tell her he'd made a mistake. She already knew that, but it was much too late for her. When he lifted her chin up to stare into her face, Kimber saw something there that she'd never seen before. Happiness.

"I suppose we should go and find our clothing and head to my house. It will be considerably more comfortable than this cold ground." Kimber looked down at him and he smiled bigger. "You're frowning. You either thought I'd yell at you, or you expected me to blame this on you."

"Yes." He nodded and pulled her mouth to his for a quick and very unfulfilling kiss. "What is wrong with you? Don't you realize what we've just done? How permanent this is?"

"Yes, I do realize a great many things. As of right now, there is nothing that we can't talk about before you think you're going to leave me. But I'm sure when I stand up I'm going to feel every rock we hit on the way down here, and my ass is going to hurt from the rock that is precariously close to becoming a part of me." Kimber thought he'd lost his mind and rolled off him. When he sat up and smiled at her, she had to laugh. The smile left him to be replaced with a look of pure agony. "I think I might have hurt myself. Can you come here and kiss them better?"

"No, I'm not going to come near you until you understand what we just did." He wiggled his brows at her. "Not that part. I mean the connecting part. Where we just sealed the deal on this thing between us."

"You mean that we're now mates. I get that, and I don't see a problem with it." She growled at him and he laughed again. "I've been around shifters before, Kimber. I know what we did, and the consequences of making love to each other. Also what the biting meant."

Kimber got up to dress as she thought of what to say to him. Turning her back to him as she pulled on her panties, she felt her heart break in pieces when things, what they'd done, hit her hard.

"Mary is not going to be happy about this. She's had her heart set on you since you first had sex with her." He asked if everyone knew they'd sometimes been lovers. "Yes. Of course everyone knew. She'd come to school or wherever and tell us what a great lover you were, and what.... That really has nothing to do with this, Hugh. We're not of the same class."

"You mean breed, and I'm fine with you being a shifter. Are you?" She growled at him again. "You're very adorable when you do that. I mean sexy too. My cock gets hard when I think of you getting all cat-like on me."

"Are you listening to yourself? You're acting like this is just going to be fine with a lot of people. They're not going to be happy with you. For all I know, they could run you out on a rail when they find out what you've done. I'm not in your class, Hugh. Don't you understand that? The castle, your money, all of it will be lost to you." Hugh asked her if she cared about that. "Of course not. It's not mine, but you lived there your whole life. Your dad was born there, as was his dad. Do you think the townspeople are going to be happy to find out that you're mated to the woman whose brother killed your family?"

"The townspeople can kiss my ass for all I care about their opinion. And I'm pretty sure that you're thinking about this too hard. No one is going to blame you for what he did. He was unhinged and hurt. I'm looking into why he might have done this. I knew your brother…this wasn't like him." Kimber didn't know what to say to him about how cavalier he was being. "I know it was much more serious than him just deciding that we all had to die. Trust me, I know that he killed with a purpose, and even tried to kill me too. But he didn't. You have to believe me when I tell you that no one will care who you are. And if they do, then I don't care about them."

She only stared at him and turned on her heel to climb the mountain that they'd fallen down. Entering the cave, Kimber knew that he was right behind her, but didn't pause when she picked up her bag and unzipped it. Finding the papers that she wanted, she tossed them at him and told him to read them.

"That one came out a few days after the slaying. 'Burton Dunn Massacres Entire McGuire Family.' Not completely true, but it did make a lot of people storm my parents' home." She threw the next one at him. "That one says we should be run out of town. Tarred and feathered, one man said, is what should happen to us. My father had a stroke after it hit the paper. He died when the local hospital refused to help him. It was horrible to have him lay there in my mother's arms and try to breathe, make the pain of it go away. Even his doctor told him that he'd have to find someone else to care for him. My parents never believed that Burton had done this on his own, but after he was killed, we didn't have anything to go on. Then after Dad died, things started to escalate out of control and we had to leave or be killed too."

"I had no idea." She told him that he'd been in the hospital himself. "I'm sorry about your father, truly I am. And I know as a result of this, you moved here, right? But this is old news to them, Kimber. I'm sure that they've changed their minds about you now."

She looked at the paper in her hand, dated three days ago. Standing up, she handed it to him as she made her way out of the cave. It no longer felt like home to her, and she wasn't sure it ever would again. Sitting on the large stone that had served as her reading place for so long, she waited for him to come out and tell her that he was going to tell Mary he was sorry. Ten minutes later, he came out with her bag and the papers.

"I'd like for you to come to my home with me. I have one nearer to my friends' house, that's where I'd like for us to go. We need to talk. And that's the only place I can think of where we won't be interrupted." She asked him if he'd read the papers. "Yes, and I think that I should have someone explain to me what they meant by some of the slander that's here, but I'll get to the bottom of it."

"None of its slander. It's all true. Even the part where it mentions that my father died poor and that we ran away in the middle of the night." Kimber could have told him word for word what had been written there. "Dad was buried in a pauper's grave because the people he worked for took everything from us when it came out that Burton had killed your parents. Even the insurance he paid into for nearly all his life was denied, the money now going to the fund for the other victims. I didn't have a problem with that, nor did Mom. We had nothing before and less than that after. But that's not what hurt Mom. It was the fact that he'd had to be buried alone, in an unmarked grave, because she'd been afraid that they'd dig him up and parade him around the town much like they had Burton."

"They did that?" She said they'd done worse. "Why? What could it have served to have done that to you and your family? You had nothing to do with the deaths of those people. There was no evidence that your parents were even aware of what he was going to do. Why would they do that?"

"They figured that one bad Dunn meant that we were all bad. Mom and I packed what little we could and headed for anywhere that no one would know us. It was next to impossible, however. Everyone knew our faces after that. So we came to the Americas." She snorted then. "The reception here wasn't much better, but at least we were able to make a living. Jobs were hard to come by, money more so. And when Mom got sick, it wasn't so much the cancer that killed her, but the fact that she'd had to leave Dad back there, and she knew that she'd never be near him again."

"I can take care of that." She told him not to bother. "I want to. And I'm going to have some words with a few people as well. Starting with Mary."

She frowned at him. "Mary? What does she have to do with all this? I mean, so far as I know, she's lived here for a long time. How would she even be aware of what is going on at home? What possible reason would she know anything about this?"

"Her father is on the board at the newspaper, and he would do anything for his little girl, that I know for sure. And I do mean anything." He handed her the paper she'd given him last and looked at where he was pointing. "That, my dear mate, is her father's name at the top of this story. I have no doubt she's been making sure he kept you and your family the targets of this since the very beginning."

"Why? I was never a part of yours or her click. I didn't hang out with any of your friends. As far as I know, my brother didn't either." He grinned at her, and she felt her cat purr at her. She was happy with their mate. "Hugh? What is it you think you might know?"

"While I had no idea she was up to this, I've been keeping tabs on Mary for a long time, and I know for a fact that this is right up her ally. She's a bitch. Might have even known it back then, but I was thinking with the wrong head. Now I'm thinking with the one that matters. Mary Manchester is trouble, and she always has been. Also, I want to find out why she is telling people that she and I are going to be married. She told Mac that on the way from picking her up. I want answers, and that little cunt is going to give them to me."

Chapter 6

"Well, he didn't come running back to me when she ran off. Hugh should have stayed there and talked to me, not left me with people I don't know. And I'm sick to death of pretending that I have nothing. Daddy, you said you'd fix this for me. I need Hugh to marry me so I can live in the big castle." Mary looked down at the newspaper that her daddy had sent her a few days ago. "You never mentioned anything about how he was getting married soon either. I want the world to know that I'm going to be the lady of the castle, and that Hugh McGuire is going to be my husband."

"Well, Pumpkin Pie, I couldn't very well say you and he were getting married without him coming there and having them fire me, now could I? And the city planners as well as the governing body decided that he could have as long as he wanted to get married, so long as he helped the little town out. You'll have time to charm him now. Bring him around. But the town, we're getting a new grade school, and the library is going to—"

"Daddy, I don't care about those things. I have no idea why you keep insisting on telling me about that stupid little place. They hated me there and treated me horribly. I've told you what I want, and you said you'd do it for me." She stomped her foot and wished that he was there to see her temper. Being on the phone with him didn't have as much effect as being in person did. "You and I both know that the will clearly states that he has to marry. How could they go against the words of his parents in this? Did you point that out to them? Tell them how the McGuires were rolling over in their graves over this?"

"Now, my little Pumpkin Pie, you know that I don't have a thing to do with that part of the town. I'm merely the newspaper man here." Mary stomped her foot again, feeling it all the way to her knees this time. If he kept making her mad, she was going to have to do something to him. "Mary, darling, look at it this way…he'll never marry the woman who practically murdered him. Not if he has any sense he won't. You just have to show him your better side. Not the temper that you're displaying now. Men like Lord McGuire do not like women who show their bad side in public."

Her daddy had not seen the way Hugh had looked at Kimber, and the way he'd knocked Mary out of the way when she tried to tell him how much she'd missed him. Then that woman had come around, and Hugh had been gone for hours before she'd heard that he'd gone home. The rest of them had packed up and left too, before she could get any information as to where home might be for him. The woman, Mac, had told her that she'd overstayed her welcome then, and had called her a cab. She'd not even had the good sense to call her a limo, even after she tried to tell her that Hugh and she were to be married soon. Mary's only consolation was that Kimber had run off, and no one had seen or heard from her since.

"Daddy, I played him just like you said I should. Mommy even told me that if I could get him just one time to forget to cover his dick, she'd make sure there was a baby for it. She even had men lined up to do the job before he was shot." Her temper started to spiral out of control when she thought of how close she'd been to convincing Hugh to marry her. And she'd be running his castle now, not letting it sit in ruin like he was doing. "Daddy, you have to do something. I'm not happy about this."

"I know, Pumpkin Pie. I know, but there is little I can do from here. I've done all that I can other than ordering him to marry you." She had wondered why he'd not done that the first time she told him that she'd been fucking the lord of the manor. "I couldn't very well get up in arms about you sleeping with him when it was a well-known fact that you'd been with a great many other men before young Hugh. Even during the time you were...that the two of you were.... People talk, darling. I tried to tell you that over and over when it was brought to my attention that you were having your fun."

"Are you saying that I'm a whore, Daddy?" He started sputtering about how he'd not said that when she felt her temper just snap. "That was all yours and Mommy's fault too. That doctor told you that had you given me more as a child, I wouldn't have had to seek out love and companionship from others. He said that I needed more than you were giving me as a little girl, and that sex was the only way I could cope. He told you that, remember? I do, even if you don't."

It had taken her giving the good doctor a blow job and letting him fuck on her the back of the couch to have him say that. Then, when he'd set up several more sessions with him, each of them ending with his dick in some part of her body, Mary had gotten a good deal more from him. A car, for starters, as well as her own credit cards that she used to this day. But it had been worth it to get him to tell her daddy that she needed to get anything she wanted. He'd also been willing to say that having Hugh McGuire as her husband would more than likely cure her desire to seek out other men. Not true, of course, but Hugh wouldn't have been any wiser about her needs than her daddy knew the truth about her and her business right now.

"Oh my child, no, I'm not saying that at all. What I'm merely pointing out to you is that my hands are tied when it comes to making Lord Hugh do much of anything. His money and his status over me keeps me in my place."

Mary screamed. Her daddy was not helping her at all. "I know what his status is, Daddy. I want it, and his money. Do you know how badly I need to be in that castle? I want people to come to Whimmpington Castle and see me there as his bride. No one else but me. Do you hear me?" He assured her that he did indeed hear her. "Then I want you to make it happen. Daddy, you said you'd do anything for me, so make this happen, or so help me, I'm not going to be very nice to you again."

After cutting him off by closing down the connection, Mary moved to the shabby little bedroom that she'd hated since she'd moved in. There was another house, not far from this apartment, where she actually slept and lived, but this one was for show. For the world to know how she'd fared after the love of her life had nearly been gunned down that day. Coming to the Americas had been her only hope of getting on with her life, or so she told those who would ask. How the hell was she supposed to know that he was going to pull through? Then when he'd arrived here a few years later, just as she was making plans to return home, Mary thought it was in the stars that her and Hugh were going to be wed and she'd be living in the big castle after all.

Mary supposed she could have moved on after Hugh had been shot, but to be honest, she was really enjoying the freedom of being here. She could fuck who she wanted when she wanted. Turn herself into anything she wanted at the drop of a hat, too.

For several months she'd pretended to be a hooker, and had even walked the streets. Well, she had been one, selling her body for the fun of it. Learning the trade and how to make it work for her had been a blast. But then the newness of it wore off when some jackwad had tried to kill her when he thought she'd held out on him when it came to letting him fuck her in the ass. She did have rules when it came to sex, and you abided by them or you didn't get to fuck her. Simple as that.

But her little foray into hooking had paid off. She had money now, lots of it, and she had to do very little to make it. Life, as far as Mary was concerned, was coming out just fine for her. And as soon as she was living in the grand castle that should have been hers all along, there would be very little else she'd need. At least for a short while, anyway.

Pulling out the newspaper again, she had to smile at her father's words. He had a command of them, for sure. But calling out the man she was going to marry for not fulfilling his part of the contract his family had had for like a million years hadn't done a thing for her. Not one single thing. The burg, he'd told her, had made him recant his harsh words, and that paper had come out with the blessing of the people for Hugh to marry when he pleased.

"Why do they need new schools anyway? And it's not

like anyone needs a library any more. Most of that shit they have in there is on the Internet. And what's not there, they don't need anyway." She read the part where her daddy had mentioned that children were needed to carry on the line, and McGuire's children needed to be running the halls there again.

"Not fucking likely. Child yes, I will have one because I have to, but no more after that. I'll have it all taken out before I'd make myself go through that more than once." She'd tried so hard to get him to forgo the condom when they'd been fucking. Not by begging, but by having him completely under her spell so that he'd forget. It had never happened. He was made of stern stuff, Hugh McGuire was.

"I've never met a man in my life more protective of his cum than Hugh was." Even today, she'd thought about throwing herself at him, for old times', sake when he'd been set on leaving her at that woman's house. Then that man had come to stand in front of her, and Hugh had told her he'd be back, that he wanted to talk to Kimber first. And no one she asked had known what had happened to him until someone said that he'd called and said he was going home.

Mary supposed that she could have lied to everyone, saying that she was having Hugh's baby back then. But that wouldn't have worked, for the very reasons her daddy had said. She'd been around a few times; even the men that her daddy had worked with had been between her legs. Mary just couldn't help herself, she really liked sex. And Hugh would have demanded a test to make sure it was his, she knew that now.

"If a man liked it like I do, then he would be told he was a stud. I'm called a whore because I like it too." She tossed the paper to the floor and got up to pace again. She'd have to go home soon, to her other place, if she wanted to get there before the entire staff left. Screaming at them for some minor infraction had kept her in good spirits for the last several weeks now, and she didn't want to miss out on that opportunity.

Calling for the car as she did every night she was here, Mary gathered what few things she'd need to take with her and started out of the little hovel she had to call home. By the time she'd gotten to the corner where Douglas picked her up, she was beginning to think of other ways she could get what she wanted. Then she saw the man standing there.

He looked familiar, but that didn't bother her overly much. She'd been fucking around too much not to at least run into one or two of the men she'd blown or had sex with. And Mary was much better at recognizing dicks than she was faces anyway. So when he waved at her, she waved back and gave him her best pose. As he made his way across the street toward her, Mary tried to think where she could take him for a quick fuck when he smiled at her.

"Mary Taggart Manchester?" She nodded, wondering when her name had sounded so sexy before. "Good. My name is Nick Stark, consider yourself served."

He shoved an envelope at her and turned away. Three men that were nearby, all with their cell phones pointed at her, started laughing. They were recording her receiving whatever the man had given her. Served, he'd said, and she knew it had something to do with being in trouble. Fuck that crap, she thought. Walking to the nearest trash can, Mary dropped it in the receptacle and blew kisses to the men.

"Won't do you any good when you don't show for a court appearance." She stared at Nick as he leaned against her car again. "You can't say you didn't get it or that you didn't read it, because we can prove that you could have, but didn't. And we all saw you take it from me when I informed you of it. And not showing for court on something this big...well, I hope you have a good lawyer. Or your daddy does."

"What would I have to do to make all that go away?" She cupped her breasts and smiled at him. "If you'd like, you can fuck me any way you want and we'll call it even. Just give me the phones and everybody is happy. Hell, I'll even fuck those guys while you watch if you want. I don't care. I just don't have time for this bullshit. Come on, Nicky, what do you say?"

"Not on your fucking life would I touch you. Christ, woman, you've had more dicks in you than the entire group of working girls on Jefferson Street have all together. And that's only in the last month. I shudder to think how many times you've had to wipe the cum off your mouth and chin." She told him she never missed a drop. "Yeah, I just bet you don't. But I'd get that envelope if I were you. Hugh will be sorely disappointed that you didn't at least read it."

He was gone before she turned back to the trash can. Each of the men were still recording her, but she didn't care. The need to know what Hugh had sent her made her reckless. Picking out the envelope, she made her way to the car as she was tearing it open. The first line on the document had her turning in the direction that the man had gone.

"You fucking prick."

Hugh was going to pay for this. Suing her wasn't going to go well for him, and this court order to keep her away from him was never going to work either; she got what she wanted or else no one did. Mary told Douglas to take her home, and to hurry. She had things to arrange.

~~~

Hugh watched as Sander paced in front of him. He'd told

94

him several times that he could find himself another attorney to help him with this matter, but Sander had insisted. It wasn't until Sander's lovely wife, Caroline, had come to his office as well that he knew they were there until the end. He had a feeling that Mary was about to get a whole bowl of shit delivered to her, and she wasn't going to like it one bit.

"I have it here that her father has booked a flight to the States. Direct, so you know that cost him a great deal of money. Money, I'm afraid, they don't have to spare." Caroline handed him several sheets of paper, and the top one had all his flight information on it. Both he and Lenore were coming for him. But the lack of funds for the Manchesters, that had come as a surprise to Hugh.

They'd always spent more than he'd ever seen a family spend on lavish vacations, as well as cars and homes. And there was the added fact that Lenore came to the States several times a year, spending money they didn't have on wardrobes and jewelry. Hugh had several himself, both cars and homes, but he only paid cash for them, and he never bought what he could not afford, and Hugh knew there wasn't much he couldn't. He had Sander look into the newspaper's books as well. Hugh had a feeling that they were going to find a great deal of their cash missing.

Kimber joined him in his office just as Sander left to do some more digging.

"How do you find your way around in this place? It's almost as big as the shopping mall in the next county." Hugh grinned at her and asked her to come to him. "No. If I do, then we'll end up having sex on that desk again, and I don't think Sander and his wife will appreciate us messing with their well-ordered stacks. What is all this, anyway?"

"Welcome to the Manchesters' life, such as it is." He

looked at the neat stacks and wondered if he could put them on the floor and then return them as neatly when he was finished with Kimber. He looked at her, and she backed away from him further. "You're not playing fairly, you know that, right?"

"We'll play later. What do you mean, the Manchesters' life? Are you thinking of taking her into your life? I don't blame you for it. She can do all sorts of things I can't. For instance, did you know that as lady of the house — that's what they're calling me, by the way — I'm required to come up with a meal plan for the week? How the hell do I know what I want to eat over the next five days? I don't even know what I want for lunch, and it's nearly time for that now. What are you doing?" He went to her then, wondering if she'd ever feel secure with him. "Don't. I'm trying to deal with all the reasons that she should be here with you and not me. I can't...I'm not cut out for this."

He pulled her to him. "She'll never be here with me. If she is, it's because I'm going to sit her down and tell her just how much trouble she's in. And from what we've found so far, both she and her family are in a great deal of trouble. Not just with me, but with all sorts of people both here and at home."

"Hanna would know." He asked her who that might be. "She used to be the cook for the Manchesters. Her mom and mine were friends for a long time before we were...we left. And she's the only one that kept in touch with her after Dad died. I think they talked once a week after we got here. I talk to her too, just to keep in the loop. You should call her."

Hugh called out to Caroline. The woman had come in very handy over the last several hours, and he wondered why he'd never known what a force she was. After telling her what Kimber had said, she nodded and got as much information from Kimber as she could. Before she left to call her, Caroline turned back to her.

"Hanna Jacobs, I think I remember her too. She and her daughter have that.... Well, I'd call it a Danish shop, but I think it's called a bakery. Is that her?" Kimber said it was. "Then we might be able to work something out we've never thought of, my dear boy. Hanna's son works at the same bank that Mr. Manchester has his account in. He might be able to tell us things that we can't get from the bank manager."

After she left, Hugh reached over and locked the door. He needed Kimber, and was pretty sure that she wanted him as well. Even after making love four times this morning — twice in the bed, once in the shower, and then in the closet when she'd been trying to find something of his to wear — he needed her again.

"You're going to wear yourself out." He laughed at her. "I'm serious. You're going to grow tired of me, then what will we have? Not much, I'm betting."

"We'll have each other. And plenty to do. Please take off your clothes and let me show you how worn out I am." The shake of her head had his need for her, roaring nearly out of control. Moving slowly toward her, he started stripping off his own clothing. "You're not going to have anything to wear if you keep denying me. Not that I don't love tearing the clothing from you, but I'm running short on things you can fit into of mine. I think I'd like you naked all the time, but there are people here besides us. Which reminds me, we have to go shopping soon. I think you have on my last pair of smaller boxers."

"I don't deny you, Hugh, you take. There is a difference." There was, he supposed, but not right now. "What do you want to do to me? Eat me? Or did you want to bend me over the desk and take me from behind?"

"Yes." She smiled at him, and he thought her beautiful. "Take off your clothing and I'll eat you before I bend you over the desk. I promise you, you'll enjoy yourself if you let me have my way."

"You are a spoiled child, has anyone ever told you that before?" He had to think, then shook his head. "You are. Trust me. Always wanting what you want. Maybe I don't want you."

"You don't want me? I don't believe that." She told him she'd never said that, she'd said *maybe* she didn't want him. "Then why are you still dressed? Is it because you want me to tear your clothing off you?"

"My cat wants you too." He paused in his movement and stared at her. He had no idea what she meant, but it sounded oh so good. He wasn't sure what that might involve. Maybe fucking her cat? That wasn't something he would be comfortable with. Did she want him to...? Hugh simply didn't know. She seemed to read his mind. "Not to have sex with her, you dork. But she needs to mark you, bite you so that you wear her mark."

Bite him. He'd seen the cat's teeth, and while they were in the mouth of Kimber, he still thought them to be big. And sharp. And huge. Hugh thought of where she might think to bite him, and wondered if this was her way of telling him she didn't enjoy sex with him.

"Where? I mean, where would she sink her teeth into me? And when she's finished, will I be able to walk? You know, on my own?" Kimber nodded, but he still didn't have the answers he needed. "Kimber? This isn't something I'm familiar with. Explain please."

"I would let her take me. Then when you were naked,

we'd lick your inner thigh and bite you there. Her saliva would numb it some. I'm not sure how much, but I know that it will hurt only a little. Then she will mark you, tear slightly into your skin so that you wear her teeth imprint. I'm not a hundred percent sure why she needs to do this, but I bet if you asked Steele that Kari has marked him as well."

There was no way he was going to bring this up with Steele, but he was considering his part in this. Then he thought, what the hell. She wouldn't kill him. At least he hoped not. Pulling off his pants, he watched her strip down as well. When she was naked before him, all he could think about was taking her.

"I need to drink from you first." She shook her head. "Please. I want to eat you now. Then when your cat marks me, I know that I can fuck you afterwards. I need you, baby."

When she spread her legs for him, he stared at the line of cream that raced down her thigh. He wanted to lick that place, taste it as it made its maiden journey down her. Dropping to his knees and making his way to her, he could smell her before he even touched her.

"Come for me. I want to feel you coming while I have my mouth on you."

Her moan had him cupping her ass and bringing her to his mouth. When she staggered slightly and held onto his head, Hugh buried his mouth over her pussy and slid his tongue as deep inside of her as he could go.

She didn't just taste delicious, it was more. Her scent along with her taste had him eating her, feasting on her as he might a meal. Every time he nipped at her, taking the hard nubbin into his mouth and eating it with his lips and tongue, Kimber rocked into his mouth. Sliding his hand up her inner thigh, he fucked her with his fingers. His hand and arm got soaked to his elbow, and he felt her every time she came, her screams echoing around not just his head but the room too. Lifting his head from her, he saw her fingers pulling hard at her nipples, her hands cupping and squeezing her breasts. When she looked down at him, her lust and need apparent even to him, she begged him to give himself to her, and he stood up just as her cat took her.

He thought he'd have a minute to prepare. At least he was sure he would. But she lunged at him, knocking him back to the floor and onto his back. Her touch, her tongue, grazed his balls and he felt them pull up into his body. Then before he could tell Kimber this was a bad idea, she bit him.

It was over in an instant. Not just the pain, he supposed, but the way that it disappeared as well. It had been harsh, brutal almost, but then it turned erotic; his cock burned with need again and he felt his balls fill, ready for her. When the big cat let him go, she snarled at him, her teeth still covered in his blood. He reached out to touch her, run his hand through her fur, and heard her purr. As suddenly as she'd become a cat, she was his Kimber again.

"Ride me." Kimber crawled up his body and he held his cock steady for her. As soon as she was over him, her heat nearly scorching him, he closed his eyes as her body took his. Her sheath swallowed his cock. And when she was seated, her body as flush with his as she could get, he rolled her to her back and fucked her harder than he ever had before.

"Come, baby."

She cried out her release and then begged him for more. As he leaned into her throat, feeling her pulse pound under his tongue, he bit down, hard. As soon as her blood touched his tongue, filling his mouth, he came screaming around her flesh as stars danced vividly behind his lids, then he simply blacked out.

Chapter 7

There was no hope for it, Bert was going to have to disappoint his little girl. She'd be upset, yes, maybe a little pissed off for a time, but she'd understand that he and her mother had done all that they could concerning Lord Hugh. He looked over at the man who had picked them up at the airport over an hour ago, and Bert thought that he might have been better off not coming here at all. Now everything was about to hit the fan, and there wasn't a thing he could do about that either. But, Bert told himself, it was going to happen sooner or later. He knew that too.

"I don't understand what you're saying to me." He glanced over at his wife of forty years and felt sorry for her. He'd kept Lenore in the dark for so many years and, now that he needed to lean on her, there was nothing left to lean on. He'd done this to her as well...made her as unaware of the real world as he could, to keep her innocent of the horrors of finance. "You can't have that right, Mr. Phillips. We have a grand amount of money. Why, just yesterday I used my credit card to buy my winter attire. You can't have the right account. I believe you need to check that again, if you please."

"I'm afraid that I do, Mrs. Manchester. In addition to your account being ceased by the banks and other creditors, I'm afraid that your home, as well as all your automobiles, have been locked down until such time that reasonable compensation can be made to all the people you owe. I would imagine that they'll gather together and see what they can sell your things for, and then—"

"No, I won't have it. Bert, tell him that this isn't right. We need our things. Whatever will our friends think when they see the locks on our doors and we're not there?" He just patted her on the leg and told her that he'd explain later. "I want you to explain now, Bert. Then I want you to tell this man to take those locks off and leave us to our business. He has no right to do this to us. We aren't even from this country. I came here to see my daughter, not to be told that my spending has to stop. I need for you to tell him that he has it wrong. Please, Bert."

"I'm afraid that everything he's saying is right. We don't have a thing, love. It's all gone now. I did keep the house up, but I'm afraid that like he said, they'll take that as well now." She started to shake her head and he nodded. "We've been... well, I have allowed us to live well beyond our means, and it's finally caught up to us. And when things started to stumble, I borrowed some from the work funds too. I'm sure he knows all about that as well. There just never seemed to be a time when I could return it, and it kept growing and growing. To be honest with you, I'm quite relieved. It was making my head and heart ache so to know that I was stealing."

"I don't care how your heart or head hurts. You'll fix this for us. I can't have my friends thinking that we're paupers. It just won't do to have the ladies of the sewing circle believing

I can't hold the next meeting because someone has taken our house from us. And what of our daughter, Bert? What do we tell her when there is no more money coming to support her?" He told her he was sorry. "Bert, you're upsetting me with this sorry business. I want to know how you plan to fix this."

"Mrs. Manchester, you are in debt to the banks for over forty million dollars. With your holdings and what little you have in your account, you are well short of paying that back. Then there is the matter of the funds owed to the company that Mr. Manchester works for. He owes them just under thirty million, plus, they're demanding that he turn over his retirement as well as all company cards and cars. As it stands now, they've cut all that off, but you still need to pay them back." Lenore was still shaking her head as Sander continued. "Then there is the matter of your daughter's accounts. I'm afraid that she is being named in the suit as well."

"Mary? What does Mary have to do with her father being a thief?" Bert felt her words as if she'd stabbed him in the heart. "She'll not be touched by this. You hear me? Our Mary is a good girl. A little on the spoiled side, yes. But she was our only child and we indulged her a little. There is no law that says that we couldn't do that, is there? You'll make sure that she's not touched by this...by her father's stupidity."

Bert felt his heart twist in his chest. Yes, this was his fault. He'd been the one that could never say no to them. But they were his girls and they had asked him so prettily. Mary was going to have a fit, he knew that. But he was more worried about his Lenore. She wasn't suited to this kind of exposure to his sins.

"No, she's not a good girl, and I'm sure you've known that for some time. She's going to jail. All of you are." When he started to ask the man if he could take all the blame for it and to leave his wife and daughter alone, Sander handed him a paper. Actually, a stack of them. "Your wife knew you were behind in your payments, Mr. Manchester. She, on two occasions in the last three weeks, told the bank manager when he called about the late payment on the house that she wasn't planning to pay him, not a penny of it. When asked why, she said that you and she were going to come here to evade the penalties until they came to their senses and let her have what she wanted. Or they'd have to try to get their money some other way."

"But I paid the house payments. Every month. It was the one thing that I made sure was paid, the house. It's all I had left of my parents." He looked down at the papers in his hand and could see that they were now five months behind in payments, as well as taxes and the credit card payments too. "I wrote out the checks myself. Put them on the...Lenore, you were to mail these in the post when you were out. You were to...what have you done? Where is all that money?"

Her entire demeanor changed. She went from his befuddled wife of all these years to a woman that he'd never seen before. Her back straightened and her eyes narrowed. Not just at him, but at Mr. Phillips as well. And in those seconds, she became this woman that reminded him a great deal of a shark and a cat rolled into one person. Someone that he was slightly afraid of.

"What did you expect me to do, Bert? Let everyone know that you're a fool? That you've no head for money and what we really needed? I had to do something or let you bring us, and our daughter, down with your ways." He nodded then shook his head, too stunned to think beyond trying to figure out who this woman was. "I had to keep our daughter in money and lovely things so she could marry Hugh. She's had her sights on that man for years, and you did nothing to get him for her. You certainly weren't helping her with that shabby apartment that you had her put in. When she needed it, she was going to get it. And since you seemed to be incapable of keeping us in the lifestyle that we have enjoyed for many years, then someone had to do it. We lose the house. So what. The cars, who cares. We can start all over. We just won't be able to go back. They won't come here to get us, so we're just as free as we were when we were younger. And not as broke as everyone thinks we are."

"But you are. Broke, I mean." She looked at Mr. Phillips when he spoke. "Your money that you've been sending here for Mary to hold for you…I'm afraid that she's spent it. Or moved it to another account that we've finally tracked down. It's gone, I'm afraid. All of it. And even that wasn't enough for her, it seems. The money would hit her bank account, the one that she had set up for you to send her money to, and she'd take it out. We've tracked down a bit of it. She has very expensive tastes. And that's not all. She's been…how shall I say this to you? Your daughter has been putting your name on credit cards and maxing them out, but never paying on them. Her place is also behind, and stuffed full of clothing and other merchandise that she's purchased. As well as personal things that she's been selling as well. But that'll be gone as well as soon as the government steps in. There will be nothing left of any of it when they get involved."

"You mean that she's been selling off her things? So?" Mr. Phillips shook his head at his Lenore and then looked at Bert. It hit him what he was saying like someone had slapped him with a large two by four.

"You mean her body? Our Mary has been selling her own wares?" Mr. Phillips looked relieved, then nodded. "My

Mary, she's been selling herself for funds? No, I won't believe that. There was money to be had. If I look at these bills that haven't been paid, there was no reason for her to do such... what on earth is she doing with all that money?"

"I don't know, sir. That doesn't appear to be her only means of support, either. There are others there as well...in her house, I mean. Other women who are doing the same thing. A houseful of them. She keeps them in line and takes a part of their...I would guess you'd call them earnings. Then, when they get to the point where they are no longer of use to her, she sends them packing without so much as the clothing they came to her with."

"My daughter is running a brothel?" He felt his heart twist in his chest as his Lenore sat there and laughed. "She's a whoremonger? My daughter, my little girl is.... I can't think."

Bert wasn't sure what to do. His wife was...he wasn't even sure what to think of her. But his little girl was running a brothel and selling herself as well. Bert realized that Mr. Phillips was still speaking when he felt the pain in his chest again. He reached out to his Lenore and she slapped his hand away.

Bert felt the next pain take his breath away. He closed his eyes when it came again, rolling over him like the water in a shower. He could hear talking, screaming really, but none of it was directed at him. Lenore was demanding that Mr. Phillips do something about her money. It was just too much. When Bert opened his eyes, he could hear his heart in his ears, and his blood rushing through his body like a freight train on a runaway track. All of him hurt, his arms felt weak. He was sick too; his belly felt ready to spew forth the little he'd eaten on the plane.

"Are you all right?" He looked at Mr. Phillips and shook

his head. His Lenore was screaming at Mr. Phillips about paying attention to her and her needs when Bert was blinded by the next pain.

He was suddenly on the floor, his shirt opened up and his wife telling him to get up, to stand up like a man, that he had embarrassed her enough. Bert was sure that he was never going to stand again, much less be anything like a man. As his vision narrowed to a pinpoint, seeing only the man standing over him pumping hard on his chest, Bert looked to his right and saw her. A woman he'd ever seen in his life was staring at him with the most beautiful smile he'd ever witnessed.

The woman was dressed in a lovely gown of gold. It was so bright that it burned his eyes. But there was something wrong with her. Her face looked...she'd been hurt, and badly it appeared. But as he watched her, her wounds faded and she smiled at him again.

"Hello there, Bert. Not doing so well, are you, buddy?" He felt his face form a grin as the cheeky woman asked him if he was ready. "We've a bit to do before you can come along with me, but I can get you going in that direction."

"Am I dead?" She told him not just yet, but he was working on it. She said that Sander was trying hard to keep him here. "I wouldn't mind so much to die. I've not been a good man."

"Sure you have…a little on the dishonest side, but a good man all the same." He saw her blur out for a few seconds, and then she smiled once more. "Sander is a good man, and he's working powerfully hard to keep you breathing. More than your wife is doing. I tell you what. You go on back to where you're lying and you help Sander. He's going to need it. And you'll be a better person for it. Go on back now, and fess up. You do that and tell them what you know about the money that you took, and you'll feel a might better in the long run. I'll be back to get you in a bit."

Nodding once, he felt his mind grasp onto something else that she told him. The woman told him to remember it. No matter what, to remember what she said to him. That he was a good man but a dishonest one, and that wasn't so bad after all. Then she was gone, and Bert felt...lost once again.

When he opened his eyes, someone was leaning over him and talking to him. He looked at the man in the blue shirt and tried to tell him he was all right. The mask over his face was making him a little lightheaded and he lifted his hand, or at least tried to lift it and remove it.

"Nah, you don't want to do that, Mr. Manchester. You need to lie still while we take care of you." He nodded and felt his belly lurch up. "Mr. Manchester, you had a heart attack, do you remember that?"

"When?" He told him earlier today. "Wife? Where is my wife?" His words sounded slurred, like he had food in his mouth. When he tried to make his mouth work again, he knew that something more than a heart attack had happened. He'd had a stroke too.

His mother had died from a stroke when he was about seventeen. Well, that was not what eventually killed her, but it was the cause for all the other health problems she had after. The entire right side of her body had never worked properly after that, and she had to have round the clock care until she died some years later...ten, as a matter of fact. Bert closed his eyes and wondered if anyone would care for him now that he was like this, and figured he was getting just what he deserved, then he let the darkness take him. But not before the words came back to him. He was a good man. A good man.

~~~

Hugh looked at the monitor again. The camera that he'd had installed in the lobby when he'd bought this building was looking right at her. Mary was sitting out there in his lobby, a place where no one other than those that worked here had ever been before. The public did not enter his domain. When he heard his name, he looked over at the five men that had come to mean more to him than anyone else had. The men he'd worked with for the last ten years.

"Mr. Manchester has had a stroke. They don't expect him to make a full recovery. His wife is currently being booked on charges that stem from her part in duping the bank and credit card companies. Mary, as you can see, has come here of her own free will, but I doubt very much that she's going to be leaving the same way. The police are standing by, as well as a few other government agencies that have to do with human trafficking and drugs." Hugh nodded at Landon when he finished. "Are you all right, Hugh? Do you need me to do something for you before this begins?"

He shook his head. Hugh was sure there were things that needed to be done, but his mind was shutting down at the moment. Things were...he supposed he could call them out of control. Way out of his control now.

"The police are raiding Ms. Manchester's home now. The women that are there are cooperating. Some of them are asking to be set free. We're not sure what that's about right now, but they'll look into it." He told Drew why they were asking for that. "Are you saying that she's brought these women here against their will, and has them now as indentured slaves? Christ, that woman is bad. Anyway, they're being booked on charges, but I think most of them will be freed by this evening. Steele is making sure that they have good representation."

They didn't know the half of it. But it, like everything

else, would come out soon enough. Sander had been very busy, and his wife was still digging into the Manchesters' lives and coming up with more and more dirt, mud really, every minute. He almost felt sorry for Bert in all this. Hugh's mom asked him when he was going to get this over with.

"She doesn't have a single bit of guilt in her body, does she, Mom?" She shook her head and touched her fingers to his cheek. He couldn't feel it, nor could she, but he knew the love that was there and told her he loved her as well. "I can't believe that we didn't know all this before. I mean, I was sort of watching her, but I never dreamed that this...she was this devious. I feel like I failed so many people in this."

"You had nothing to do with this, son. Not a damned thing. Bert is somewhat responsible for the fiasco of his daughter. But I'm as shocked as you on what Sander has dug up about Lenore. She seemed so...well, I never thought she was right in the head, to be honest." Neither had Hugh, and he said so to his dad when he continued. "And I'm sure that was why she got away with things for so long. And she taught her daughter well, apparently. Never heard of such a thing. Not in all my life would I have...well, I'm just glad that they're about to have an ending to this."

When the phone rang a few minutes later, he was watching Mary while she primped as someone answered it. He'd seen her do that a lot when they were younger...make sure that her hair was just so, her breasts tucked up so that they showed off her ample cleavage. It had always amazed him that she cared. Not that he didn't think that she should try and be pretty, but that she was wasting her efforts on him. He had thought her beautiful back then.

"That was Sander. The house has been taken. The accounts are frozen, and the Feds have gathered up the computers in both her homes as well as the two in her office. Connie and Aster were able to lead them to the ones she had hidden in the basement, as well as the safe she had down there. It's all done." He nodded, not taking his eyes from the woman that was going down in a few minutes. When Steele cleared his throat before continuing, he looked at him. "Hugh, I'm really sorry about this."

"It's all right. I knew it was going to come to a head sooner or later. I just didn't know that all of this would come out." Hugh had yet to tell him the worst part. He wasn't even sure how to, but he turned to the group of men and his parents and let out a long breath before he could begin to even speak. "She put a contract out on Kimber's life two days ago. And I've not told Kimber yet, but she...but Mary.... This is going to be a shocker to you all. I just found out that she was responsible for Burton coming to the office that day and killing my parents and shooting me. She told him that we were responsible for Kimber dying, when in fact the conversion had saved her. She may or may not have known about it when she told Burton that we caused her death, but I'm looking into that as well. Mary wanted Kimber dead to use her supposed death to fuel Burton into doing what she wanted. To kill my parents so that I'd be left the sole heir to the house and everything in it. Mary had ordered the nurse to kill Kimber sometime during the week when she told Burton. Changing Kimber was the nurse's idea when she realized that Kimber wasn't nearly the person that Mary said she was. I think that's why Mary knew that Kimber was a cat when she saw her that day."

He saw his mother fade away. Then his father, a very strong man, stood there staring at him for a long while, until he, too, left them. There was more, a great deal more, but he was pretty sure that his parents might get more information than he had on what had happened that day. Looking at Drew, who had been his best friend forever, he could see the shock and disbelief on his face.

"It was her plan to have my parents killed so that I'd inherit everything. She wanted it all. Not necessarily me, but the things that I could give her. The castle, the money, and the status that she felt should have been hers all along. And her mother, Lenore, was right there with her when she told Burton that not only had we murdered his sister by taking away any and all support that she needed to live, but we had already picked out the grave in the paupers' section of the cemetery. She told him that Kimber had meant that little to us." He heard someone cursing and he thought it was Mitch, but he wanted to tell this before he met with Mary. "The day that Burton got into the building, someone had fixed his badge so that he could...his badge had been deactivated when he'd been terminated. But Mary had...she'd gotten one of the men that she'd fucked to change it back. Blackmailed him to fix it, or she'd tell his wife. The man later killed himself when Mary let it be known that not only had she fucked the man, but his son as well. The boy is mentally handicapped, and her story destroyed the man."

"Did he tell you this? The guard, did he give you this information?" Hugh nodded at Steele, and told him he'd only just talked to him. It had never occurred to him before that Mary was involved. "And Burton, have you been able to talk to him? To see if this is true or not? Not that I don't believe you, but damn, it would be nice to have someone tell us why she did this."

"Money. And no, I've not talked to Burton. I can't seem to find him." Steele said it had to be more than just money. "What do you mean? Isn't that a good enough reason to kill?

114

We've certainly seen enough of it in what we do."

"Yes, we have. But this sounds too planned for it to be just money. There has to be...something there. Something you've missed." Hugh started to ask Steele what the hell it could be when Steele's sister appeared in the room. "Can you find Burton Dunn for me? I think he might have gone on, at least that's what we assumed. Use everyone if you have to. This is important."

When she left, Steele told him it was time to deal with Mary. He had no idea what Steele thought Aster was going to find by talking to the man, but he wanted this over with as well. As soon as he went to the door to get her, everyone in the room, with the exception of Drew, hid in the adjacent office to watch and listen. Asking her to come into his office was the hardest thing he'd ever done to date, he thought, when all he wanted to do was throw her from the top of the building.

Mary paused in the doorway when she saw Drew. "Oh. I wasn't aware we were going to have company. Hello. I think I might have seen you at Hugh's house the other day." Drew said it was his house and he did not remember her. "It was the day that we found out that Kimber was a cat. Surely you remember that? Then she ran off and Hugh left me there all alone. Hugh, honey, you shouldn't do that to your guest."

"You knew she was a cat all along, Mary. And as I didn't invite you to the house in the first place, I saw no reason for me to see to your needs. But that's not why I'm meeting with you. Please have a seat and we'll get started." He could see that she hated being called out, but right now thought she was lucky that he didn't strangle her. Instead, he pulled out the file that had everything she'd been up to for the past twelve years as soon as she sat down. "By the way, did you know that your dad is in the hospital? He had a heart attack then a stroke this morning, and your mom was with him. From what I understand, he might not make it."

"Oh no. Poor Daddy. He always did work much too hard. I tried to tell him all the time to slow down and take care of himself. Is he going to be all right? I've seen where people who have strokes never quite recover. I just don't know what I'm going to do being here and him sick all the way over there at home." When she pulled out a tissue and dabbed at her eyes, Hugh looked over at Drew. This was going to be better than he thought. At least for him anyway. "Maybe you could go back with me, Hugh, in your jet. I know that Daddy would love to see you again. He always had a soft spot for you in his heart."

"As you well know, I don't own a jet. And your father is here, in the States. He and your mother arrived earlier this morning, and were talking with my attorney when he had the stroke." She looked confused and glanced at Drew for some sort of confirmation. Drew just smiled at her, one of those kind smiles that are not too terribly friendly looking. "Your mom has been arrested too."

"My mom? She did that to him, didn't she? Upset him again so that...I knew that she hated my daddy. The heartless woman. Hugh, I cannot believe that she'd do this to him. We have to make sure that Daddy gets the best of care. You'll do that for him, won't you?" Hugh asked her what she thought her mom would have done. "Why, I'm sure I don't know, but Mommy isn't as innocent as she lets on to be. That's why I came here. To get away from her."

"You came here because this is where I was. And the townspeople were ready to string you up. Taking advantage of the very people that helped you is not a very smart thing to do in business circles." She looked pissy, and then dumbfounded. Had he not been looking at her when the change overcame her, he might have missed it. "But as far as your daddy is concerned, I think he's the most innocent of the three of you. At least in most of the shit I've been able to uncover about you and your family. You have been a very busy person, haven't you, Mary?"

"Whatever do you mean?" She laughed; it was forced, and he could see the beads of sweat forming on her forehead. When she pressed her handkerchief at it, he could see her hands trembling as well. Hugh didn't even feel bad for what he was doing to her. She deserved this, and so much more. "My daddy is a good man who would do anything for me. As for my mother, she has her moments of usefulness. But as far as coming here to escape the people of the town, they were just jealous of our relationship, and they couldn't stand the fact that you and I were a couple."

"We were never a couple, Mary. You were just some woman that I fucked. Nothing more. And your dad did a great deal for you, didn't he, Mary? Robbing from his employer to help you stay here as you continued going about your life the way you had at home. It cost him a great deal, you know. Then your mother…it was a real surprise when we found out that not only was she stealing from her own husband, but she was helping you fund a pretty good sized business too. How many women have you had working for you at any given time, Mary? Forty? Fifty? Are you still hooking yourself? By the way, it really sent him over the edge when he found out that not only was his little Mary still spreading her legs, but now she was getting paid for it too."

"Hugh, I will not stand for you treating me this way." She stood up and sat back down when he barked at her to sit. "This isn't like you. What sort of things has that animal told you? You can't believe a single word out of her mouth, you know. Her family...well, you know what they did to you and yours. Kimber's brother killed your entire family, Hugh. Certainly you've not forgotten that, have you?"

"No, I can't forget that, but I do know who to blame now. And it was never Kimber, and poor Burton was just a pawn. I want you to know that I found out you told Burton to come there that day. Supplied him with the gun and the access to come into a building that he'd been barred from. And after telling him that not only had his sister died, but that we had been the ones that had caused her death, you practically put him in a cab to go there with your blessings, didn't you? You told him that we took away her only means of living, and now she was dead." Mary looked at Drew, then back at him. Her laughter, a small forced twitter of a sound, made him smile. "But that's not all, is it? I have so much more to impart to you today. Mary, I take great pleasure in informing you that your whorehouse is now under siege by the federal government. That all your money, even the offshore accounts, has been taken as well. Also, when you leave here, you'll be taken into custody for not just prostitution, but for the trafficking of humans, money laundering, and the manufacturing, as well as the distribution, of drugs. You will also be charged in the murder of my parents, the attempted murder of—"

"You can't do that to me." He didn't say anything as she stood up. "You and I are going to be married, and you cannot do this to your wife. Hugh, I have been planning this for a long time, and now is not the time for you to be finding this shit out. I have a plan. I need you to marry me. Damn it, you know that you're not going to get any better than me. And I know how to run that castle of ours. I am going to run that castle. It's mine. You hear me, that castle is mine. You'll have to have them drop all these charges right now, and tell them that you've made a mistake. Put my money back, too. I worked hard for that money. It won't do for your wife to have this hanging over her head."

"I'm already married." He waited for her to look at him, then showed her his wedding band. "As of nine this morning, Kimber and I became man and—"

"That animal? You married that animal? You can't be fucking serious. Christ, Hugh, am I going to have to do everything for you? What did she tell you, that she was pregnant? I can have that taken care of. I have a man on staff at the house who knows more about a woman's plumbing than most doctors do. But you are not going to be married to her. I won't allow that. I want you to call the proper people now and have this taken care of. I'll wait. You go ahead and do this for me, and I'll try my best to forgive you." She sat down and looked at him. Hugh had to admit, he was sort of speechless after that. "Well? What the fuck are you waiting for? She needs to be gotten rid of right now. I can't believe after everything I've done for you, you have the nerve to do this to me. You will have to do some major groveling for me to forgive you for this, Hugh, my darling."

"Well, I guess it really sucks to be you then." They all turned to see Kimber standing in the doorway. She was smiling and looking at Mary like she was the piece of trash that she was. "Mary, you aren't going to like prison one bit, I think. And I, for one, am glad to see you going there."

When she stood up, knocking the chair back, Mary lunged at Kimber like she meant to harm her. But Kimber changed into her cat quicker than he could see. It was over before he could stand up and Drew could clear the table.

"Get this thing off me." Hugh had to hang onto the table

while his heart got under control. "Hugh, darling, this is not going to sit well with me. Get this animal off me right now."

Kimber had her by the throat, not gently either, if the trickle of blood was any indication. When the others joined them in the room, Steele started laughing first, then the rest of them. Christ, it was perfect. And while they were waiting on the police, Mitch and Landon started snapping pictures. He guessed that they would be to the families before Mary was in cuffs.

Mary was still screaming when the police took her away in cuffs a few minutes later.

Chapter 8

Nick was beside himself with worry. When they'd called him back to the room where Addie was being examined at the doctor's office, he thought they were going to tell him that she had another few days to go. He didn't think he could last that long. Addie was four days overdue, and he was scared the baby was stuck or something. But when he'd gotten back there, they told him that not only was she in labor, but had been for a while, and that they were shipping her to the hospital immediately. Then Landon had called saying Dillon's water had broken, and they were headed in too.

Now they waited.

"Do you suppose they had the babies already and forgot to tell us?" James had come with him, as the two of them were supposed to go pick up some food after the doctor's appointment, and have a family gathering at his and Addie's house. "I would think that with two babies coming at the same time, they might forget."

"I doubt that the women would let them forget about

us." Landon was pacing up and down the small room, and Nick wanted to tell him he wasn't helping. "Besides, we're supposed to go back there too when they have them prepped. Whatever the hell that means. I'm pretty sure that being in labor is about as prepped as you can get."

"I don't think that's what they mean." Kari told Landon to sit down before she put him down. Then she looked at Nick. "You seem really calm. I'm glad. You can be a little intense when it comes to Addie."

"Intense? Okay, maybe, but she's overdue and I'm worried about her a little." Kari assured him that four days was not that much. "You have no idea how...well, maybe you do. She's been a little cranky the last few days. And that nesting thing has been driving me nuts. Did I tell you that she organized my glove compartment? There were three things in there, and now they're in small little snap closure boxes labeled with a tag on them, and not just put in alphabetical order, but she keeps checking to make sure that I don't put them back wrong. It's three things, Kari. Three."

Her laughter put him at ease. The nurse came down the hall and he and Landon stood up. As Landon was being led away, he watched to see if someone came for him. Addie was here first was his way of thinking, and should have been ready before Dillon. But when the doctor, one that he'd only seen twice when Addie's own doctor was out, came walking down the hall, he felt lightheaded and dizzy. He knew that something had gone wrong.

"Mr. Stark. We need to talk. Would you come to my office with—?" All of his friends gathered behind him, both living and dead. Then one of them put their hand on his shoulder. "It really is a private family matter, sir."

"They are my family. What you have to say to me, you can

say to them as well." He thought that if this was bad, someone would need to help him. His legs were already shaking.

"The baby is large, as we told you several weeks ago. And now...well, now he's in distress. The cord is wrapped around him tightly. Not just his left arm and right leg, though that is bad enough, but his throat as well. We're worried that as labor progresses, the cord could do some damage to his extremities if it doesn't strangle him first."

Nick felt his body simply let go. He could hear them, Steele talking to the doctor, someone saying his name over and over. He heard Aster speaking to him as well. Then when Mitch slapped him, his hand raised to do it again, Nick began to focus. He grabbed Mitch's hand before he connected once more and thanked him, knowing that without the hit, he'd be in the corner sucking his thumb about now.

"I need to see Addie." The doctor said that she was being sedated; she had not taken the news well at all. "Well no fucking shit, you moron. You just told her that our son is hurt, and he's not even born yet. Take me to my wife."

"Sir, you don't understand. She won't be able to—" Vinnie lifted the doctor by his neck and shook him twice before she put him back on the floor. Then she told him that he was going to do as he was told, or she'd make sure that he was never heard from again. "All right. I can...this is highly irregular."

"You have no idea."

He saw Aster and Billy in the room first. Then he saw Connie and Carlton. They were all there, standing close to Addie and watching over her. When he approached the bed to take her hand, he could see that she was indeed drugged, and he asked no one in particular what that was doing to their child.

Aster answered him when the nurse started prattling on about heart monitors and IVs. "He's doing fine now. A little upset, but he's doing well. You need to fire that idiot and get someone in here that knows what the hell they're doing. That man is a moron, and needs to stop hurting babies with his ways."

"Why? What has he done?" They all looked at each other, then back at him. "Tell me. I'll need a better reason than he's an idiot and a ghost told me to do it."

"Did you say something, Mr. Stark?" He turned and looked at the nurse standing there. "He said to get her ready for labor and delivery. I don't think that's going to work for either of them."

"What do you mean? Get her ready? He's going to have her give birth naturally?" She nodded, then shook her head. "Nurse Rachel, I'm a little stressed right now. So if you don't mind telling me what you meant, I won't get a headache and hit someone. Everyone will be all right, and we all might survive this."

"If she tries to deliver that little boy, he's going to die, and she will too. He's too big, and with him all wrapped up like he is, there will be hemorrhaging. A lot of it. She's exhausted now, and if he does this, which he's ordered me to do until someone tells me differently, your wife and son aren't going to live." She looked around the room as if she wasn't aware of what she'd said. Aster left her body then and winked at him.

"I only told her to tell you the truth. Not the version she's told others that had this same idiot." He looked back at the nurse, who still looked a little shell shocked.

When the door opened and the doctor came in, Nick knew that if he didn't act now, he was never going to get another chance. Standing in front of Addie, he told the doctor to get out. It was perhaps the scariest thing he'd ever done.

"What do you mean, get out? I'm the doctor in charge, young man, and if you don't get out of my way, I'm going to call security." The doctor turned to the nurse. "Why is she still not ready? I'm ready to deliver this child, and she's not even prepped."

Nick hit him. It was a bad move all the way around, but Nick picked up the tray that was nearest to him and slammed it into the man's face. As soon as he fell, his face bleeding all over the floor, he turned to Aster.

"Get me a doctor. I don't care if you have to take his body and bring him here, get him." She nodded and disappeared. Nick turned to Billy. "Find Steele and the others. Tell them what is going on and what I've done. Someone might have to bail me out of jail when this is done."

As soon as he was gone, Nick looked at Rachel. She simply went to the phone and pressed two numbers. Nick wanted to cry. He just could not live without his Addie, and if they tried to take him out of here, there was going to be hell to pay. A lot of it.

"Doctor Nellie is at it again, sugar. Can you call up the team for me?" Rachel turned to him as she listened to someone on the other end. "Yeah, Mrs. Stark is in trouble here, and we need a surgeon on standby too. And please hurry. Nellie is bleeding on the floor...yes, he was...he fell over one of the cords and now he's out like a light. Yes, that's the story I'm gonna stick to. Have Sherman doctor up those recordings too while you're at it."

As she hung up, a doctor looking completely confused entered. He asked Rachel what was going on and she told him. The new doctor, Anderson his name badge said, took the clipboard and read as she explained. No one, not the doctor nor the nurse that came in a few minutes later, asked about the man on the floor.

Within five minutes, Addie was being wheeled to surgery and he was being taken to be questioned by the head of the department. He had been told that due to the nature of the procedure he couldn't be there. Well, fuck that shit.

"I'm going in there." The woman that had no name badge started to lead him away, her hand on his back, her other hand reaching for his. Nick pulled away from her and stretched his neck. "Make it happen, or so help me, I will not just own this hospital in ten minutes, but I will have your job and your retirement in my pocket. I'm not fucking around now. Do it or walk."

She stared at him, and he knew the moment that someone walked up behind him. He didn't have to turn to see who it was. Steele had a presence that surpassed needing to look. The man simply exuded strength and power.

Nodding once, she told him to follow her and he was led down the hall. He'd never been so terrified and overwhelmed in his life. He was glad when Steele reached out and grabbed him as he felt his knees give out.

"Steady there. I got you."

Nick knew that he had him in more ways than just holding him up. He felt his eyes fill with tears, and before he could stop himself, he leaned into the big man's chest and sobbed.

"I can't lose them. I just...I love them both so much, I just can't lose them now." He cried harder, his heart breaking at the thought of going in that room to be told he was too late. "Steele, what am I going to do?"

"Buck up and get your ass in there with your wife." He looked up at Steele and tried to think if he'd ever heard him use that tone before. "You want me to tell her that you're a whiney assed baby and couldn't be bothered to see your son being born? Huh? Is that what you want?"

"No. Of course not." He felt his temper flare up, and he glared at the man that he'd been ready to die for only moments ago. "You're a real bastard, you know that?"

"Yeah, I know. But you love me." Steele hugged him tightly before shoving him away. "Now, seriously, get your ass in there and help bring that little boy into the world. He's going to need you as much as Addie does."

When he was dressed in the clothing they handed him, he made his way to the operating room. He was ready, he told himself. His wife needed him. There was a little boy there who would too. But as soon as he entered the big sterile room, he heard the doctor shouting.

"We're losing her."

~~~

Drew sat quietly while Aster told them what had happened only moments ago. Nick had a son, but his wife might not make it. Aster said that they had waited too long, delayed the delivery just enough that now Addie was the one in trouble.

"He's bruised around his neck and arm. His leg too, but not nearly as bad as his little throat. They're putting him the NIC unit now to keep a closer eye on him. Nick is with Addie." Drew figured that was where he'd be. He would be too. Standing up, he went to the front desk, Mitch and Hugh right behind him.

"I'd like to be able to go in and visit the Stark baby, please. And before you tell me no, you should know that I can and will put a world of hurt on this hospital that will only be rivaled by baby Stark's dad." He shook the anger off his body and tried again. "I don't want to cause him any trouble or stress. I won't touch him in any way. But I want to be with him, for his dad, while his mother gets better."

"I'll see what I can do, Mr. Mullins." When she turned and left him, he held tightly onto the counter and waited. If anyone had asked him what he was thinking about, he wouldn't have been able to tell them, he just waited for the nurse to return. "You can go in one at a time and sit with him for twenty minutes each. Don't touch him or any of the equipment around him. And when the nurses tell you to move, you'd better be halfway across the room before they finish the word. You understand?" They all told her that they did.

Drew sat next to the tiny bed that held the little boy. He had a mask over his face and a tube running in his nose. Drew watched his little chest move up and down around his own mask, while wearing protective gear that stuck to his skin like it was glued there and felt itchy and hot, but it was for the little boy, not for his comfort, he knew that. The room was hot, hotter than he'd ever been in, but Baby Stark, as they were all calling him now, needed it warm rather than cool. There was what appeared to be an IV in his tiny belly, and several tabs of some sort on his chest.

Several machines were at his head. One he knew was monitoring his heart rate, which seemed to be strong. Another, he was told, was keeping an eye on his body temperature. That too looked about normal, if not a little high. The nurse there with him explained that it needed to be warmer, as they didn't want him to get a chill. When he was finally alone, or as alone as he was ever going to get in this room, he leaned over and began talking to the little boy.

"Your mom is a fighter. I don't want you to worry about her not coming through for you guys. I've never seen a more

128

stubborn or pigheaded person in my life. Unless, of course, you count your father. Man, that guy can be stubborn when he wants to be." Drew thought about what he was saying. "Not to say that they're not the nicest people in the world. I love your dad like a brother. More so, I think, than most would their own sibling. And your mom? She is something else, that mom of yours."

He watched the little guy's chest go up and down, and thought of his own children. "James is doing well. You'll get to know him better when you grow up. I would imagine that you'll love him as much as I do. And he's doing well in school. Better than they thought he would with all the crap he'd gone through getting to us. Straight As, and he's been asked to be on the debate team. He's really good to his sister too. Becky is walking on her own now, and should be running by spring time. She's already calling us Mom and Dad. You have no idea what that is going to do to your parents the first time you say it to them. It melts the heart, so say it often."

The nurse came and checked on the baby, then smiled at him. Drew knew that the baby couldn't understand him, but he wanted to tell him about the family, the huge overbearing family, he had come into.

"Steele. There's a lot to be said about him. He's a good man, a better father than most, and he loves with all that he is. And your parents. They're wonderfully strong too. I'm thinking that with your parents' background and all, you'll be strong like them. But Steele is everything in the world to all of us. He'll be hard on you when he thinks you need it, but right there if you need that too." Drew smiled when he thought of Kari. "She's a cat, a panther shifter. And I'd be careful about making her mad at you, not that you will. I have a feeling that like her little girl, Aster, you're going to have her wrapped around your finger too.

"Mitch is married to Vinnie, who is a vampire. You don't have to worry about her either. She's a wonderful woman, and a great friend to us all as well. Mitch had his problems for a time, but he's doing much better now. I think it helps that he's got Vinnie. I know how much Mac has helped me out.

"Let's see. Landon. He's a great person. Loving and well balanced, and he and his wife, Dillon, are just down the hall bringing their new baby into the world." He tried to remember if anyone had been told what the sex was, and figured it didn't matter right now. "You'll have yourself a playmate in his baby. Might be a girl, but that's all right. Girls are pretty good at baseball and stuff. If anyone gives you any shit...crap about playing with girls, you just introduce them to Mac. She's better than most men I know, and the best wife a man could ask for."

The nurse told him that she needed to roll the baby over, and he watched as she took the little guy up in her strong hands and moved him to his other side. He asked her why they did that, and she told him it was to keep him from getting fluid in his lungs. Nodding, he sat back down with the baby.

"Wish I could hold you. I know that they're saying that you need to be stress free for a little while longer, but I think holding you would do a lot for my own stress level." Smiling, he thought of what Addie would do to him if she knew he'd held her son before she had. "The doctor that delivered you said that you were a strong fighter. I just hope you let a little of that stay behind when you left your momma."

When his time was up, he moved to the outdoors instead of going to the waiting room. He needed air, fresh air that didn't smell of sickness and medicine. He knew the moment that Connie joined him.

"That was a very nice thing you did in there for Nick." He asked her what it was he'd done. "Sit with his son. Talked to him the way his dad would have. Even telling him about the men in his life and how they'd be. I suppose we shouldn't be jealous that you didn't mention any of us."

"I only had twenty minutes. I'm gonna work on you guys when it's my turn again." He grinned at her when she laughed. "Have you been to see Addie yet? Is she any better?"

"The doctors are doing all they can for her. She's got the best care there is to have. All of them men you told her son about have called in favors and got her what she needs." He nodded and put his face up to the night sky. "We found Burton."

He felt his body chill at the name of the man who had murdered his best friend's parents. When he asked her where he was, she only shook her head and waved him off. Wherever the man was, it wasn't a good place, he'd bet. Not that he didn't deserve it, but he'd been a pawn in the entire thing.

"Have you told anyone else?" She said that she'd not, there had been babies coming. "Yeah, that should be a happy time, not a sad one."

But it was turning out to be. If Addie died...he didn't want to think about what would happen if she passed away. Nick was strong, but this...he thought that if anything happened to Mac, he'd just curl into a ball and join her.

"I didn't tell him that his sister was alive yet. He's in a very dark place, and I'm not sure that having her alive would do much for him. He is carrying some very heavy burdens." Drew told her that he might come out of it if he knew. "I don't know. I think he'd be better off seeing her, not just hearing about her. He might go over the edge if he finds out that he's been lied to and...I don't think Mary will live long enough

131

to stand trial if he finds out what she's done to him and his family."

Mary was currently in jail, not prison, where she belonged though. They had put her there so that she could go and visit her father if she wanted or if he called for her. It was easier than bringing her all the way across the state if either of them needed each other. Bert had refused, even in his very poor health, to see his wife. Lenore was all right with that, but she did ask to see her daughter. He had a feeling that there was going to be more plotting going on between them, and he would just as soon they never got the chance.

"Has the judge said whether or not they can meet?" He'd bet that no one wanted those two women together. They were dangerous, and deadly. "I hope that they both spend a very long time in jail over this. They've ruined a great many lives."

"Bert talked to Sander. It was difficult on the poor man to make him understand, but he finally got it. He claims to have talked with a cheeky woman who told him he had to come clean before he died. I don't know what he said to Sander, but soon after he left, Bert slipped into a coma. They don't expect him to come around again."

Bert had been stealing from his own company for years, trying to provide more for his family than they deserved, and when he'd had a stroke, neither his wife nor his daughter seemed to care much about him other than whether his insurance was up to date. Drew wished he could have been in the room when they were told that wasn't going to happen. That the policy, like everything else, was going to repay the stolen money. These women were as greedy as they came.

When he made his way back into the hospital, he stopped by the NIC unit to see how Baby Stark was doing before going to see about Addie. No one had heard anything since he'd

132

left, and Drew sat down with the rest of them.

At a quarter to seven, nearly ten hours after Landon's little girl had been born, both mother and baby happy and healthy, Nick came down the hall. He was smiling and crying at the same time. And when he picked him up and swung him around the room, Drew thought for sure he was going to have broken ribs. But he knew that any pain would be worth it if the news was good.

"She just opened her eyes and asked me to see our son. Told me that I had to go and tell you guys first that she was fine as rain, and then bring her our boy." He hugged them all two more times. "She's fine. My Addie is fine."

When Nick left them, Drew sat down. He was so happy that he could hardly breathe around it. Saying up a small prayer of thanks, Drew knew that things were going to be better for them all.

Chapter 9

Hugh wasn't sure what he might find down in this building, but he had come with Carlton and Billy and felt a little better. Connie was with Burton right now, and waiting for them to arrive, she said that Burton was more afraid then he was. Hugh didn't think that was even possible. It seemed that she was the only person that he'd talk to or even let see him, and she'd gone ahead to prepare him. Hugh had made sure she let him know that he just wanted to talk, nothing more. Connie was shaking her head before he could have her ask him if he would see him.

"I don't think you understand, he wants to go over, but is terrified of his fate there." Hugh could understand that. He'd done some pretty horrific things while alive, and there would be consequences for that. "He won't even talk about Mary, not even to let me ask him about what she might have said to him that day."

Now here he was, going to talk to the man who had put a bullet in his head, along with killing his mom and dad.

135

Hugh didn't think he'd ever forget the look on his face that morning. The look of rage that had his eyes glazed over and his gun steady in his hand.

Connie was standing there when they got to the lowest level of the building. There was someone standing next to her, a big hulking person, but he wasn't sure it was Burton until he turned around. Hugh stopped walking just to stare at him.

"Grief. Even the dead have it. Took me many a year to get over the fact that I was dead." Hugh looked at Carlton as he continued. "I know it's not the same for this poor fellow, but he's hurting all the same. Loss of his sister, at least in his mind. Then the murders he's carrying around. Can't say that I blame him for doing what he's doing."

"And what is he doing? I mean, he's here for a reason… what is it, Carlton?" The man moved closer and Hugh followed him. Just as he was within a few feet of Connie and Burton, he saw it. "Holy Christ."

Every inch of the place was covered in chalk drawings. Not many of them were good, but Hugh could make out the faces well enough to know that they were of him and his parents. There were some of Kimber too. He had no idea how he'd gotten them there…more than likely he'd taken over a body here and there and had them come here and draw for him. He figured that was why some of the drawings were better than the others.

As he stepped closer to one of Kimber, Burton moved to shield it from him. As they stared at one another, Hugh had a feeling that Burton might not remember who he was. When he had been killed by the police, as far as he knew, Hugh had died along with his parents. When he took a staggering step back, Hugh said his name.

"You can't be here." Hugh nodded and told him he was,

and that he wanted to talk to him. "I don't talk to anyone anymore. To her, but she's pushy, and I can't get away from her."

"Connie? She is pushy. Could you have imagined meeting her when we were both alive? I'm sure she would have straightened our asses out, don't you?" Burton smiled and nodded. It didn't last long, the smile didn't, but he stared at him now. "I have some news for you, a lot actually. If you'd not mind, I'd like to ask you a few questions as well."

"I killed them and you for what you did to my family." Hugh had already figured that part out. "I shouldn't have done that. I know that now. But...she was all I had in the world, my Peach, and I just couldn't...I should never have done what I did."

"Kimber...Peach is alive, Burton. In fact, she and I were married just the other day in the courthouse." Burton began shaking his head. "Yes, she is. Mary lied to you. Well, she actually thought she was telling you the truth, but the nurse that was supposed to murder Kimber for Mary couldn't do it because she had grown fond of her."

"No. Mary said that she was dead. That you and your family took away the support she was getting, plus, the medicines and things she needed. It was all that was keeping her alive." Hugh told him again that Mary had lied to him. "She showed me her body. Took me right in that room and let me see her...I couldn't touch her though. Mary said that you had said if I did, then you'd not even bury her properly."

Hugh pulled out the picture of Kimber with today's paper in her hand. She was going to come and see her brother after he talked to him, but for now, he hoped this would help. The man stared at it for several seconds before he looked back at him.

"This is a cruel thing you do. I know that I've done you wrong, but there is no reason for you to hurt me this way. I've paid dearly for what I did to you. But it was only what you deserved." Nodding, Hugh pulled out his phone. Dialing the number that he had gotten for Kimber yesterday, he put it on speaker.

"Burton? Are you there?" Her voice echoed around the room. "I can't hear you, but I can talk so you can hear me. And Hugh said he'd let me know what you say to me. I'm here, Piglet. I'm alive."

He had told Kimber to think of something that only the two of them knew. She said that when Burton would come and read to her, which he did almost daily, he'd call her Peach and she'd call him her Piglet. It must have worked, because Burton was sobbing hard as she continued to speak to him.

"Piglet? Please trust my husband. Sounds weird saying that, but he is, and we're happy together. But we have to finish this with Mary Manchester. Do you remember her?" Burton said that he did and Hugh told her. "Oh good. Not a very nice person, Mary. But I'm thinking you might have figured that out on your own. Anyway, I'd very much like for you to tell Hugh what she said to you that day. And what her mom said."

"She was there, that mother of hers." Kimber said that she knew that too. "They told me that you were gone. Said that... they told me that you were dead, and that the McGuires were responsible for it."

"I'm fine, Piglet. I promise you I am. And when you're ready, I'd like to see you. Well, I can't see you, but we can talk, you and me." Burton asked Hugh when he could go and see her.

"Now if you want. But I really do want to find out what

138

she told you." He nodded and said he'd give him whatever he wanted. Even tell him where the films were. "Films? You mean you recorded the conversation with her?"

"No, not me. That…when Peach got sick, the doctor put in one of those monitor things in her room. I could go to my computer at work and watch her during my day. I'd not sit there all day, but I'd make sure she was getting her meds on time and all that stuff." Hugh nodded, his heart going triple speed. "When I was…when the police came to the building and chased me out…you know? Anyway. I figured I'd better prove to someone I was justified in what I did to you and your parents. I went there first and got all the tapes I could find and hid them. I never got to go and get them later."

Hugh asked him where they were. When he had the location, he hung up with Kimber and called Steele. Christ, tapes. If they were any good, he'd have her up on murder charges as well as all the other stuff she had in her file right now.

The reunion went better than he could have hoped for. Steele had gotten the video tapes, all that was really available then, and had someone going over them now. And he was with Kimber when he and her brother showed up. As soon as Burton saw her standing in the middle of the living room, the man simply broke down.

"Tell her how sorry I am. Tell her…tell her how much I love her, and that I'm so very sorry." Steele walked to the man and asked for him to take his hand. "Yes, I'm ready to go now. You can…everyone has heard of you. Even me, with my hiding out all this time. Just make sure that you tell her that I never have stopped thinking about her, and that I — "

"Take my hand, Burton, and you can tell her yourself." He didn't look as if he was going to trust him. Or perhaps it was something else. "She loves you as well, and would like nothing more than to hear your voice one more time before you move on. Take my hand and she can see you. This other, we're going to clear your name too. Not that you didn't kill people in cold blood, but you were grief stricken, and we're going to prove that. Take my hand and talk to your sister."

As soon as their hands touched, Burton burst into tears, as did Kimber. Even Hugh felt the tug of his heart when they talked over each other, telling one another how much they had missed them and how dearly they had loved them.

~~~

Mary wasn't sure what she was supposed to do with herself. She was positive there had been some sort of mistake in all of this. And as soon as her daddy got out of bed and came down here to fix things, she was going after Hugh again. Daddy shouldn't just be lazing about when there were things to do, and she was going to tell him that. To think that Hugh thought to lie to her about having a wife.

"Not her."

The room was empty, but for her. There was a camera hanging over the cell just out of her reach, but she didn't bother with that. Most of the time they were just for show anyway. She had them all over her house.

Her house. She'd been able to see some of the news story on her. Not once did anyone put up a picture of her, nor did they come here and ask her what was going on. And those women she had working for her had said some really terrible things about her. Most of them were just unfair. True, but as she was unable to defend herself, Mary thought that people shouldn't just jump to the conclusion that she was in the wrong.

A person had to make a living. And so what if she had

acquired these women in to help her reach her goals? They had a nice room that she paid for, plus, food and clothing. There was no reason for them to say she'd brought them here without their consent. Okay, she hadn't gotten it, but again, without her there to defend herself, they should know better than to say it. Hugh had a lot of work to do, cleaning up the mess that was being made over his future wife.

The person coming down the hallway was whistling again. She had no idea why no one had yet pointed out to her before this that she was terrible at it, but it mattered little, it seemed, to the police woman. Mary had tried to tell her several times over the last few days that she didn't want her to do it, but she did it anyway. Mary thought perhaps she was doing it to be mean. Everyone was mean to her now. That was going to change as well.

"Miss Manchester? I have some news for you." Mary told her she had news for her as well. "Your father passed away this morning."

"You need to stop whistling. I've mentioned this to you before. You can't carry a tune for anything, and it's getting on my last nerve." She asked her if she'd heard what she said. "Yes, he's dead. I need for you to contact Lord Hugh McGuire. He's the Tenth Lord of Whimmpington, and has a lovely castle that I'm going to run soon. Tell him that my daddy is dead and that I've sat here long enough. He needs to get off his ass and get me out of here."

"I'm not sure you understand, Miss Manchester. I just told you that your father passed away, and you're acting like it was nothing. You're not getting out until the trial, either. And I'm not calling Mr. McGuire for you. He's made it clear that he wants nothing to do with you." Mary stood up and told the woman to do it. "I've only just come to tell you that your father passed. The rest isn't going to happen."

As she walked away, whistling again, Mary started to scream at her to get her ass back here. When she didn't, Mary added her name to the long list of people that Hugh was going to have to straighten out. Mary sat down and tried to think what she was going to do now. If her daddy was gone, then who was going to bail her out so she could go to Hugh? No one, it seemed, was helping her.

In actuality, this was her daddy's fault anyway. All of it. Had he just done what she'd wanted a long time ago, she'd be married to Hugh and then she'd have the castle and servants she had always wanted. Even all the cars were supposed to be hers, and would have been had her daddy just made Hugh marry her when she'd told him that she'd been fucking the man. Then she had to take matters into her own hands, which was what got people killed. All because her daddy had no balls.

He'd told her that with her reputation that no one would believe that she was having a baby of the lord. First of all, he'd explained to her, everyone knew for a fact that the young man had always used safe sex practices, and secondly, Mary wasn't really a peer of the lord and lady, and it was highly unlikely that they'd accept her in the family should she get caught.

"So? I like sex. Why does that have to figure into this at all? Why don't you just pay them all off, Daddy? Make them keep their mouths shut, and I'll make sure that he fills me with his seed." Her father had blushed brightly at her words, and Mary remembered thinking what a prude he was. But he told her that there wasn't enough money in the world for him to pay off all the people that she'd slept with and expect it to stick.

142

"And now look, here I am in jail for something that anyone would have done to get what they wanted." Leaning back on the bed so she touched the wall, she thought of her mommy. Christ, she was useless to her now as well.

Her mommy and her had plotted and planned for months before she'd left for the States. If she were to come here, where Hugh was, she could find him, get knocked up, and marry him here, her mother had told her. No one would question the baby then. The people here would be none the wiser of her inability to keep her panties up and her legs together.

They sold off everything they could get their hands on. Her mommy's jewelry. The cars that her daddy didn't use much. Even going so far as to lie to the police about how they'd come up missing so that they could put a claim on the insurance and get that money too.

Then there was the money that her mommy had started sending her. Her mommy had figured out that she could skip a few payments, four it had turned out, and then make one so the bank never contacted her daddy. Even the credit cards were very flexible when she started keeping that money as well. Making a payment once in a while to keep the creditors off her back had given Mary a great deal of ready cash. All the while, Mommy would send that money to her, and Mary was supposed to put it in the bank so when they were caught, and they would be, there would be fall back money for them to use. But Mary needed it more, and had started using it for herself. Her parents, she told herself, would want her to have anything she wanted.

Mommy had even gone to the stores, charged up the maximum amount she could daily, then taken the stuff back a few weeks later for cash. They'd ordered expensive items online, then told the stores that they had never arrived, that no one had seen the boxes that were to have been left. The money was just pouring in.

The plan had been to make herself look good. Rich and successful. But that hadn't worked out well either. There were just too many pretty things she wanted to save much for anything. Then she'd come upon the idea of selling herself. That had worked out well too. Money was coming in again, and that was when Mary had hit upon the idea that she could get others to work for her and pocket that money as well.

"Now this bullshit."

Standing up, Mary looked down the hall to the large mirror that hung there. She could almost see all of the front rooms, but nothing of the other cells. Her mother wasn't here, or so she'd been told, and she wanted to ask her what she was going to do about getting them out of here. Or at least Mary out. Her mommy wasn't really important to her plans of getting the big castle other than her money.

Then Mary saw him. Hugh had always had a way about him. It was his walk, her mommy used to say. He swaggered just enough to make you think he had his body together. But Mary had seen his body, and he had his together just fine. Mary thought it was his airs. Not the kind that he breathed in and out, but his money and his poise. He had been born to be rich, and he did it better than anyone she'd ever seen. And he was all hers. Forever. Just as soon as he cleared all this stuff up.

"Mary. These men are here to talk to you." She nodded and asked him what he was there for. "Nothing, other than to see your face when you answer them. I had no idea that you were so devious."

He'd made it sound like a bad thing, but she didn't take it that way. "Thanks. I have had to work harder than you know to get things just the way I want them for you and I. When are you going to get me out of here, Hugh darling? We have a lot of planning to do before we go back to my castle. Are there still servants there? And cars for me to be driven around in? I'd really like to get started on the redecorating. Your parents were nice and all, but they had no taste when it comes to making me happy." He told her that she wasn't going anywhere with him and she put out her lower lip, something she had practiced in the mirror a lot over the years. "Now, Hugh, you know that we're meant to be together. Otherwise all this was for nothing."

"It *was* for nothing, Mary. As I said, I'm only here to see your face when they tell you all that we've found out about you. You have been very busy." She nodded. There was no way he'd be able to keep her from him. Mary really had worked very hard at this, and she was going to get what she wanted.

The man standing next to Hugh started telling her that she had rights.

"I know I do. And the right to not be here is being violated." Mary reached out and ran her finger down his shirt front, wondering why he didn't have on a tie. She so loved to be tied up with a man's tie. "Why don't you get rid of all these other stiffs, and you join me in here for a little fun time? I think we could really make this room rumble, don't you?"

He stepped back and she had to laugh. Men were so stupid. Did they really think that women didn't know what to do get them to do whatever they wanted by showing them a little tit? And they'd sit up and beg if you gave them some pussy. She waved him off when he asked her if she wanted an attorney. Hugh was here now, and if she needed one he would be sure to tell her.

145

"Miss Manchester, on the day that Mr. Dunn came to you about his sister's health, did you or did you not tell him that she was dead?" Mary said that she had. But of course that had been a mistake, she'd been lied to. "Did you also tell him that the McGuires were responsible for this alleged death?"

"Now why would I do that? Hugh's parents had provided very nicely for the Dunns. They'd even hired a full-time nurse to go in and care for the girl. I think you should look into the nurse too. I think she might have had something to do with this whole thing." Nodding, she smiled at the man and shook her head. "You do know that Burton had been unstable for most of his life. He could barely hold down a job, from what I've heard. And he was abusive to his family too."

"You're sure? You never had a conversation with Burton, telling him that not only had the nurse that the McGuires hired been fired, but that all financial support had been taken away too, directly causing the alleged death of Kimber Dunn, his sister." She didn't care for the way he was wording this. It was almost as if he knew just what she had said to Burton. "You're sure?"

"How many times are you going to ask me that same question? I had nothing to do with Burton going all ape shit over the death of his sister. The only thing I said to him, over the phone, was that she was dead and that I was terribly sorry. Burton and I go way back, and I hated that he'd lost her. Or so we had thought. Who knew he'd go to the McGuire offices and take it out on a bunch of innocent people?"

"You did, but no one ever knew the reason he went there. You just admitted that you did." She looked at Hugh when he spoke. "You were recorded telling him that, standing over the bed that Kimber was in. Your mother too was standing there, blocking Burton from seeing his sister too closely, or he might have realized that you lied to him. It also shows that not only did you tell him a lie about the nurse, but about the support my family was still providing for her. And you also gave him his employee badge, a new one that had been printed and activated by the man you fucked behind the desk so he'd make it for you."

Her world was crashing, and she needed a minute to think her way out of it. But she knew that no matter what, if she came clean, she was never going to get him to marry her. Instead, she smiled at him to buy herself some time. Then it hit her.

"Kimber did this, didn't she? Had you come in here and lie about some recording you have? Oh, Hugh, you've been duped. I would never have done anything like that." The man that had asked her if she was sure handed her a picture. A sheet of them, as a matter of fact. And on it were six pictures of her and Burton and her mother standing over the bed of Kimber. "This could have been taken at any time. Kimber was...is my friend too."

"There is a time stamp on the tapes. All of them. We even have where you commissioned the nurse to kill young Kimber and put her out of everyone's misery, as you said. You knew that the woman had a drinking problem, and even provided her with the alcohol that you hoped she would drink down and be open to your suggestions. But you failed to understand or even bother to find out, Shelly Patrick had long since given up drinking, and was as sober as you are when she converted Kimber rather than let her die."

Mary dropped the pictures and backed from the cell door. "I need time to think. I have to come up with a good enough reason why you'd have these things against me." Hugh asked her if she was going to lie again. "Well of course I am, you idiot. I'm not going to jail. I'm going to marry you and take the castle for my own."

He laughed at her, and she failed to see the humor in this. When she told him that, he laughed all the harder. It wasn't until the other men joined him and she stomped her foot and told him to stop it that he looked at her. For some reason, Mary had a feeling he was really looking deep inside of her.

"You drove an innocent man to murder for you. My parents are both dead, Burton is dead, and your father is as well. And for what, Mary?" He moved back from her, not just in distance but out of her reach. "All in the name of greed."

He was leaving her here. "Hugh, you can't do this to me. I did this for us. For me. Come back here, damn it. I said to get back here."

Mary sat down. She had no idea what she was supposed to do now. But she did know this...if she couldn't have the big castle and all the money with Hugh, then no one would. She screamed for an officer to come to her and stripped off her clothing. Time to make some payback.

Chapter 10

Kimber realized that everyone was quiet, and she pulled herself from her memories. Most of them weren't all that wonderful anyway, and she was glad for the distraction. Looking at the women who had come to the house to be there for her while Hugh went to deal with Mary, she wondered how she'd ever thought she could be one of them. A woman of power who could command households.

"Would you like to hold her?" Nodding, she reached for the little pink bundle. For the life of her she couldn't remember the name that she'd been told, and looked at Dillon when she laughed. "Britney Elizabeth. I can't decide if we want to call her Bri or Beth. But Landon said that there might be some confusion with calling her Beth, as that's Steele's mom's name."

"Bri is good if you go that way. I like it anyway." Kimber pulled the blanket down off Bri's little hands, and put her own finger close enough that Bri could curl her fingers around it. "She's beautiful. I mean, I know you are aware of that, but she

149

is very beautiful."

Bri looked a great deal like her father. Dark hair that had just enough hints of red in it to make you think that she was going to be cursed with freckles. Pretty lips that were full, and right now stained with her mother's milk, moved as if she were still nursing, but she was sleeping soundly. It was hoped that she'd be like her mother in that she could find things and people, and also like her daddy in being the best necromancer around…next to Steele, that is.

"We think so too."

Kimber looked over at the baby in the arms of Addie. Both baby and momma were sleeping, the two of them still worn out from all that had happened to them. With a whisper, Dillon told her that she was doing much better.

Addie had come home the day before yesterday, much to the dismay of her doctors. But she told them there was shit going on at home and she was needed. Besides, she was pretty sure that no one at home was going to let her overdo it, and might be sterner than the nurses would ever be. They all had taken turns helping her with the new baby.

Nickolas Simon Stark looked a great deal like his mom, and had the temperament of his father. Laid back, easygoing until he was hungry, and had put up nicely with being cuddled and cooed at.

Kimber looked up at little Aster when she toddled over to see her. Baby Aster had not liked her at first. Her cat, Kari told her, was different than hers, and she wasn't sure how to react. Kimber hadn't had a lot of interaction with small children. When she'd been younger she'd been sick, and other kids hadn't been invited over. The only person that she'd spent any real time with was Burton, and he'd been much older than her when he'd been alive. But a trip to the toy store had brought young Aster around, much to the amusement of her parents.

Kari came in and plopped down on the chair next to her before speaking. "That was Sander. He said to tell you that everything went better than planned." Kimber nodded and asked Kari if they were coming back now. "Not yet. They have papers to file, and Steele wanted to go over the monthly schedule again. I think they're going to have to hire a few more people to come and help them if business keeps up this way."

Hugh was thinking of leaving the team too. They had talked about it a great deal, and he said that with things going on at home, there was a need to get the little burg that his parents had watched over for so long into shape. Buildings needed upkeep, and several other projects had been brought to his attention when he'd told the city planners that he was married now.

Kimber had no idea how to be rich, and had not one clue of how to run a house as large as the one that Hugh had grown up in. This one, only about half the size, was giving her nightmares on what to do and not do. She didn't know how to shop, had no idea how to manage a staff, and if Hugh ever wanted to have a dinner party, she wouldn't have the first clue on how to make it happen, much less organize the food and drinks. It was frightening how poorly prepared she was to be a lady of the castle, quite literally. She thought perhaps she might pay attention to the others to get some ideas, but they were so good at it that all she'd been able to do was be impressed.

Vinnie and Mac came in a little later. They had been called out to deal with an unwanted presence in a house, and since it had been late enough in the evening, she'd taken Vinnie rather than going alone. Kimber wondered if she'd ever feel that comfortable with these women to ask them to help her out when she needed it.

When Vinnie sat beside her, Kimber took a deep breath and looked at the vampire, surprised.

"Yeah, I know. Caught me off guard too." When Mac asked her what was going on, Vinnie blushed deeply. "I'm going to have a baby. I've not even told Mitch yet, but I guess other supers, like you guys, can tell the difference in my scent."

Everyone was happy for her. Kimber and Hugh had never discussed children, but he wasn't using any kind of protection. Not that it would matter much to her kind; the only sure fire way for a cat to not get pregnant was for him not to have sex with her at all. Condoms rarely stayed in one piece, especially the way they had sex. But she also knew that she wasn't in heat as yet, and thought that had better be something high on their list of things to talk about.

"You guys remember that woman that offered to have a baby for us? Well, it turns out that she's going to have a baby of her own now, and she has decided not to keep it." Mac nodded when they told her that they were sorry. "No, don't be. Drew and I have decided that either way we'd take another child, but we really wanted a baby this time. Oh, and there are two little boys coming to live with us next week. Ray found them living in an abandoned housing project after their mother passed away. So we might have a houseful at Christmas."

Christmas. She'd not had a real one in a very long time. Looking around the big room again, she wondered if Hugh would want to put up a tree, or prefer to be at his home for the holidays. Either way, she needed money to get busy on some shopping. There were babies to buy for, and she loved the large toy department at the mall.

Rosa Sosa, their new cook, came in to ask them if any of them were staying for dinner. Her husband, Tomas, fussed at her for doing his job when he entered the room behind her and asked them again. It was decided that they were much more entertaining than television, as all they did was fuss and pick at each other. When tea was decided on and Tomas said he'd be back with it, Kimber handed Bri back to her mother and stood up. It was past time for her to explain a few things to these women before they figured it out on their own and made fun of her. Maybe they still would, but she had to explain.

"My mother and father are gone, as you know. My dad, he was a good man…stern, but loving. My mom loved him with all her heart, and when he died, it left a big hole in her heart." Mac said that she could understand that. "After Burton was killed and I had been changed…things got really bad for us. I mean…I'm not saying that Mary had anything to do with it, but after the townspeople dug up Burton, it hurt me and my mom. They displayed him around town, going so far as to take turns putting him in their yards so that they might piss on him whenever the urge hit them. I think that was why we worked so hard to go away. The shame of it all was just too much on my mom."

"I'm sure Mary had plenty to do with that. They're finding out more and more about her all the time. That chick had some serious penis envy when it came to that castle of Hugh's." Kimber thought so too, but didn't comment on Vinnie's suggestion. "What is it you need for us to do, Kimber? We're family now, and we all know how rough you've had it. Let us help you."

"I don't know how to do this." Kari asked her what she meant. "I don't know how to be any of this. Like you guys, poised and proper. I think I'm going to fall on my face the first time I have to do something for Hugh, and he's going to see me for the dolt that I am."

No one said a word. She looked at each of them and thought perhaps she'd not explained it very well. Then Vinnie started laughing, followed by Mac and Kari. And finally Dillon, and the now awake Addie. Kimber started for the door, thinking that she would rather live alone.

"Wait." She turned and looked at Kari as she wiped at the tears. "Oh honey, I'm sorry, but I think we all thought it was funny that you think we have this shit together. Christ, we're all fumbling through this like blind mice, trying to get a clue about where the cat might be."

"No. You're all so put together, and you know how to talk to your staff and get them to do what you want."

They all turned to Tomas when he took that moment to wheel in the cart. He asked them if they needed something more.

"No. We were just discussing how underqualified Mrs. McGuire is to run this household. What do you think?" He looked at her then back at Kari, and asked her if it was a joke. "She seems to think that she has no idea how to be in charge of a household like this one. Has she been fumbling through keeping up?"

"No, she's been a little hesitant about things, but I think perhaps that's a good trait, as she thinks before she speaks. Mr. McGuire, he is the same way. Thinking first and not letting things get out of his control before he lets you know what he wants." Tomas looked at her and smiled. "You have never once given us any indication that you are fumbling,

Mistress. Quite the opposite. You are kind, generous, and very well mannered. And when you have given us things to do you have been polite in asking, not making demands on us as others have. I think I should like to work for you for the rest of my days, if you don't mind."

"I'd like that as well."

He left them then, forgetting about the tea cart and the goodies on it. Kimber didn't mind serving, and thought perhaps that was what he'd thought her to do. As she sat down to pour, she looked at Kari when she said her name.

"You're going to fit in with us perfectly, you know that, right?" Kimber wasn't so sure, and said that to her. "Oh no. You're going to be just fine. Great, as a matter of fact."

~~~

Hugh found Kimber sitting on the deck when he returned home later that night. She wasn't sleeping, he knew that, but she was so still that he paused, not wanting to disturb her. But she started talking, and he moved to join her on the patio furniture.

"They come out every night, don't they? The deer, I mean." He looked out where she'd been looking and saw them now. A male and three does, along with what appeared to be five or so young. "I didn't think they'd come out with me here. But the big guy, he keeps an eye on me."

"Because of you being a cat?" Kimber nodded and looked at him. "I didn't want to bother you. Only to let you know I was home."

"I could smell you." That threw him off a little, and he nearly smelled himself to see if he stank. "No, it's because I'm a cat. I have superior senses now. Like I can see further than you. As well as smell things that humans wouldn't. Like, I can tell that you had a lemon in your tea today. As well

155

as something chocolatey. Not too much of the latter, but you did. I also know that you pumped gas—it's on your hands—and you might have brushed up against a cat, not me. Maybe Steele. He'd smell of Kari, and you smell of them both now."

"I did have tea with lemon. I don't drink it often, but when I do, I like a little zest in it. I had a bite of a scone that Nick brought in today. Dark chocolate. Not my favorite, but I tasted it all the same. I didn't get gas, just hung up the pump when Mitch brought me home." He grinned. "Can you read my mind too? Because that would really save some time if you did."

"You want to fuck me." Startled, he sat up almost as soon as he'd laid back. Her laughter had him frowning. She was scary at times. "No, I didn't read your mind. I could if I wanted, but no, I didn't this time. You can mine as well if you'd like."

"How? And why?" She told him. "So, because of the blood we exchanged, we can read each other's thoughts, as well as hear one another too?"

"Pretty much. I can call to you, same as you can me. I can find you too. I'm not so sure that works in the reverse for you. I can smell deeper, as I've pointed out, so you might not be able to find me as quickly." Hugh nodded, thinking this mate business was very helpful. "I can also smell you when you're aroused."

"Really?" She asked him where Tomas and Rosa were. "They went home when I got here. And so you know, we're going to have to hire more staff soon. They were telling me that they can do this, but being alone here is too much on them."

"All right. I'll need help with that. I haven't the first clue on how to hire anyone." He told her that he could get his staff to run checks on them, and she could go from there. "I'm supposed to tell you that I'm a moron about this household stuff. That's not what Kari said exactly, but I am. I don't want you to ever be ashamed of me when we are out and about."

"That's never going to happen. And I'm very proud of you. This is difficult on me as well, so you know. My parents took care of most things…all of it, actually. I'm learning, but I have to have help as well." She nodded and looked out over the fields. "I would like to go home soon. After this is all over. Is that all right with you?"

"I'm afraid to, if you want to know the truth of that." She looked at him. "I got a call today, telling me that my mom has been moved to the family plot in England. And a marker has been put up for them both. Thank you for that."

He didn't say anything. Hugh had made a few calls and had it taken care of a few weeks ago for her. There were other things in the works as well. Most of them were going to affect them long term, and some not so much. Sander had helped him draft a new will, too, before he and his lovely wife had left for their first of many stops. And now Steele was helping him find a new attorney, one he would trust as much as he had Sander.

"Kimber, I've not said this to you before, but I'm in love with you. I think I have been for a long time." She didn't answer him, and he felt himself get nervous. "I want to have children with you. Lots of them, as a matter of fact. I would like for us to be the lord and lady of the castle, and raise our children to be the kind of people my parents would be proud of. I'm in love with you."

"I'd like to shift and run you down in the woods." His cock stretched painfully in his pants. He laid back again, this time rubbing his cock with his hand to soothe it. "Take off your clothes and run ahead of me. I want to hunt you, like prey."

"Will you hurt me?" She shook her head and stood up. As she began to strip down, he watched her, his body responding to each article of clothing she took off. "You have the most amazing body. Sleek and hard, yet soft and supple as well."

"My cat does that. She's stronger than I am in a great many ways. And because of her, I have a healthy appetite, as well as a hunger that burns in my belly for you." Kimber tossed her blouse to the floor and cupped her bare breasts. "I love you too, Hugh. I have since the day that you came to my cave and got all macho on me. I will never love anyone again, so I've given it all to you. Forever and always. But all day I thought of you, naked, running through the woods with me chasing you. I'll find you, of course, but it's the thought of finding you naked that has me wet and achy for you."

"Shift for me. I want to see you do it."

Nodding, she pulled her tear away pants off, panties and all. When she stood before him in all her beauty, he was tempted to tell her to come to him, but her cat took her.

It wasn't just a matter of her shifting from one form to the next, it was as if they consumed the other until there was nothing left of their counterpart. There didn't seem to be any pain for either of them. No messy, bloody shift, but a simple taking of one to the other. When they were done playing, he wanted to watch her cat let her go too. He felt her touch his mind only seconds before she spoke.

Strip for me, Hugh. Let me see your cock before I leave you here. Standing up, he pulled his T-shirt up and over his head. His body, he knew, was in good shape. The kind of work they did, as well as the fact that he ran seven miles a day, kept him fit and toned. But having her watch him this way, as her cat, made him slightly nervous. So he began talking, just to stem his fear.

"One day—and not just yet—I want you to convert me. I know that it'll be painful for me, but I want to run with you, as you are now." Her nod made him feel encouraged for the next part. "I want us to have children, as I've said. Soon too. I know that you have to be in heat for that to happen because I had a talk with Steele today. But when you are, and if you want, I would very much like to create a child with you."

I'd like that too. I'm not in heat. I don't know how my cycle works, but it should be soon. Now that I have a mate, I'm to understand that it will be more frequent than it was before. He nodded and sat down to pull off his socks and shoes. *Are you by chance teasing me?*

"I am. Sort of." He put his shoes under his chair then stood up. "I'm a little nervous, if you want to know the truth. I have no idea what to expect from this. I know that you won't hurt me, but you are a big fucking cat."

She shifted back, her sleek cat gone, and Kimber now stood before him as herself. His breath caught at how quickly she'd done it, and he could only stare at her as she dropped to her knees and unsnapped the top button on his jeans.

"I've thought of tasting your cock again. The way it feels when you slide in and out of my mouth." As soon as she had freed him, he nearly cried out when she took his crown into her mouth and swirled her tongue around it before taking the rest of his cock into her mouth.

"Christ."

Hugh fucked her pretty mouth with his cock. He wanted to be gentle with her, not hurt her mouth, but the more she moved her tongue over and around him, the harder he rammed his cock into her. When she swallowed around him, her throat tightening, he put his hand to the back of her head and held her there for several seconds. It was an amazing feeling, to know that he was down her throat like this and she was enjoying it as much as he was. When he moved again, this time hard punches to her, he did cry out when she cupped his heavy balls in her hands and gave them a none too gentle twist. His climax raced down his spine to his balls in record time, then out of his cock.

Hugh held onto the railing when he was complete but as she continued to lick and fondle him, he felt himself get hard again, his body ready for anything. Pulling her up, he turned her to the railing this time and bent her over it as he slammed his cock deep into her pussy.

"Come for me." She shook her head, and Hugh reached up and grabbed a handful of her hair, jerking her up and to him. "Come for me. Scream out your release so that everyone can hear you."

She did come, her body bowing back to his. Her hands cupped her breasts as she cried out again and again, each climax making her strangle his cock as he fucked her over and over. When she begged him to stop, her body too tired to go on, he kissed her shoulder and held her to him until his own heart stopped racing.

With his free hand, he slid his fingers into her pussy. She was soaking wet, her cream heavy and thick in her pussy, and he pinched her clit twice before he bent her over again. This time, with his fingers at her pussy and his cock in her sheath, he took his time with her, fucking her like he had all the time in the world. He knew that any minute he was going to come again, but for now, he wanted to see to her pleasure. And he had the added advantage that he could watch her beautiful breasts bounce in time to his cock, and he loved it.

He loved her. Telling her and hearing her say it back to him had lifted a great weight, one that he'd not known he was carrying, off his heart. He was in love, something that he had been sure he'd never have in his lifetime. But Steele had told him that he'd never know how she felt if he didn't ask, so that had prompted him to tell her just how he felt in his heart.

Leaning over her, he kissed her spine where it met her neck. Then he licked the dewy sweat from her shoulder before he bit her. Not hard, at least he didn't think so. But when she tightened around him, telling him to do it again, he tore at her shoulder as hard as he could until he tasted her blood.

She came then. Her hand reaching behind her and pulling him to her body, he fucked her hard, his cock straining to come again. When he did release, his cock spewing out his cum, Hugh told her that he loved her, and would for the rest of his life.

He lay over her, his body spent, his mind for once blank of all the millions of thoughts that came to him. When she giggled, he lifted his body as best he could and told her to behave.

"I love you as well." He smiled, his body feeling stronger by the second. "You are far and away the most amazing lover I've ever had."

Standing up, he swatted her on the ass, then kissed her. "I'm also the only one you've ever had. And you should know that it's very impolite to laugh at a man when he's just given you numerous climaxes."

"I'll remember that for the next time." He told her again that he loved her. "And I love you, very much. So much that I'm thinking that we might be able to make this work. Don't you?"

"I do. I honestly do." As they dressed, kissing and

touching each other, he thought of all the things that were going to happen in the next several weeks. He wanted it done, and he was pretty sure Kimber did as well. Moving on had never held much of an appeal to him until he'd met and married Kimber. Love was grand, he thought.

Chapter 11

Mary just stared at the man in front of her. So far all he'd been able to help her with was...well, nothing. He kept going on and on about how she needed to be prepared for her trial, and was not answering her questions. Putting up her hand as well as she could with these stupid chains on only pissed her off more when he didn't shut up.

"Listen to me." He finally stopped talking and looked at her. "I want you to tell me when I'm getting out of here. I have shit to do. A lot of it. And I want you to tell me when Hugh is coming to see me again. I need to have him get me out of this."

"Ms. Manchester, as I have said, several times now, you are not now, nor are you ever, getting out of jail. You'll be lucky if they don't give you a lethal injection for all the crimes that they have against you. You have to listen to me when I tell you that your only hope of not being killed by this is to plead guilty to lesser charges." Mary asked him what she'd done wrong. "Are you kidding? You conspired to commit murder. Murder. Prostitution. Money laundering. They have you for racketeering, for...Ms. Manchester, you are not going to get away with this list. Not ever. Your best bet is to hope you have a judge that thinks you're insane."

"I am not insane." She'd had a long talk with a man yesterday who said he was there to test her. "He was a queer, did you know that? No matter how much I tried to get him to fuck me, he kept telling me to back off. Why would a man turn down that?"

"Perhaps because he has values." She knew men better than that. And if she wasn't chained to the table by her legs and arms, she'd show this little shit how much she really knew. "There is also another charge of you trying to bribe a guard by offering him sex to be released."

"He wanted it as much as I did. I could see his cock getting hard when he saw me. Then he had to scream like I hurt him or something." He hadn't really screamed, but he had called for his fellow officers. She hadn't cared that there were more than one, but they just stood there laughing at her. And making fun of her attempts to get them to fuck her. "Why are people not realizing that I'm going to be lady of the castle soon? I mean, even you sort of treat me like I'm not above you in the realm of things. Why is that?"

"Perhaps because we all see you for what you are. A pathetic woman who has ruined other people's lives without regard. Killed to get what you think you should have. And gone on as if nothing affects you. Which I might add, I don't think things do. You see what you want, and you take it. Not caring at all for those you might hurt on the way."

Mary laughed. "And? What's your point? You can't tell me that you've not done the same thing. A man like you, one that has no looks at all, barely educated, I would imagine, and wears a wedding ring as if someone like me would believe that you're married. You expect me, or anyone else for that matter, to believe that you didn't trample on a few people to get yourself a job like representing a person of my stature?" He said nothing to her. "I'm not going to need you once Hugh finds out what's been going on here. He may not like me right now, but that's okay. I'm going to make him see that I am the only person for him and his money. He'll see me the way I meant for him to. A woman who doesn't take no for an answer, and that I work hard to get what I want. He'll realize that when he tries to make Kimber his lady. She won't have a clue what to do, and the first time she embarrasses him, he'll come running back to me. You'll see."

The man—she had no idea what his name was because she didn't really care—started gathering up his things and putting them in the leather briefcase he'd brought with him. It had been a nice touch, that case. But not enough for her to not see right through him.

"I'm married and have four children. I graduated top in my class. Not the top ten or even five, but first at Harvard. I own my own company, pay my bills on time, and I don't have to do this." He stood up. "Hugh is not going to come for you. He wants nothing to do with you or anything that you have going on in that small minded head of yours. You are, Ms. Manchester, going to rot in a jail cell for the rest of your days, being fucked up by women that won't take your shit any more than Hugh did."

"Oh, boo hoo. So what, you leave me here? I don't need you any more than I did my parents." She thought of them now, her parents, who had never loved her enough to give her what she wanted. "Tell Hugh that I'm still waiting on him to come here and get me out."

He left her then, the man with the nice briefcase. The woman in the uniform, who had stood so still in the corner while she talked to the man, came toward her then, and told her to stand up. When Mary did, all she could think about was that people were going to regret treating her this way. As she was led back to the room—Mary refused to call it a cell—she wondered what Hugh was doing and if he had missed her yet. As soon as she was in the room and unlocked from the chains, Mary sat down and told the officer she was ready for a bath now.

"Good for you. You got yourself a nice sink right there and some soap. I'd suggest you wash yourself in parts, as the hot water doesn't last all that long around here." The officer then started down the hall and Mary told her to come back.

"I want you to take me someplace to shower. I can't use this sink, and that soap is not even scented. Get me some of the kind I had at home. I'm sure you have my things in a box around here. Go there and get it, and my shampoo and conditioner." The officer just stood there. "You heard me. I need to have a shower and my things. This has gone on long enough, if you think you're trying to teach me some sort of lesson."

"Lesson? Oh honey, you have no idea the sort of lessons you're gonna be learning in a few weeks. When this trial of yours is done and over, you're going to go away. To a prison where they eat women like you for breakfast, lunch, and dinner. And I don't mean in the pleasurable, sexual way. Though I bet that happens too. But you ain't gonna enjoy it, no sirree. You're going to be screaming for that mommy of yours at the top of those pampered lungs." Mary told her that it was never going to happen. "You keep right on thinking that, little girl. Right up until they take you on that big bus and drop you off in the middle of what I like to call dumbass hell."

Mary sat down on her bed. That woman had better be bringing her the things she wanted. There was no way she was going to wash up again like she'd had to do yesterday. Mary was not going to be happy if they didn't get on the ball.

"You should be dead." The voice, much like her daddy's, sounded right next to her head. "I'm gone because of you and your mother. You should be dead as well."

"Daddy?" Mary got up and looked around. "Where are you, Daddy? They told me that you were dead. I should have known it was a lie. I want you to come and get me out of here, Daddy. I have had enough of this crap. You and Mommy need to get me out of here and figure out a way for Hugh to marry me."

"You love him?" Love? There was no such thing, and she told him that. "I see. So all of this, this planning that you had me be a part of, you never loved the man, only wanted his money?"

"And his castle. Don't forget that. That is going to be mine, and when it is, you'll be wishing you'd helped me sooner." She smiled when she thought of the things her daddy could do for her. "They took all my money, so I'm going to need for you to figure out a way to get me some more. And make them give me back my house too. I know you don't approve of what I was doing there, but it was mine and they had no rights to it. Hugh will need to be brought around too. You tell him that I'm going to be his wife soon, and that he'd better own up to his responsibilities."

"As you have done?" Mary asked him what he meant. "Your responsibilities. Have you owned up to them? The fact that you murdered his parents and that boy, Burton?"

"I had nothing to do with that, Daddy. You know that. Burton was a little unstable." She smiled. "Okay, he wasn't until I pushed him, but all I did was fabricate a little fib, and he did the rest."

"You brought him the gun and told him that he had to make them pay." She had done that as well, but she'd not pulled the trigger, had she? "Those people would be alive today but for you and Lenore's lies. And he nearly killed young Hugh. Then what would you have done?"

"He wasn't supposed to hurt Hugh. I don't even know why he was there that day. Hugh never went to the building downtown. It was why I waited to talk to Burton when I knew that both his parents would be at work." Mary thought of Hugh being hurt too. "If he had died, everything I worked for would have been shit. Burton nearly messed everything up."

"I think you did that all on your own." She said nothing to him. Her daddy never got things right anyway. Mary asked him when he was coming to get her out of this place. "I'm not. I'm dead, as you have been told. But unlike you, I've been able to redeem myself a little by telling them about offshore accounts and everything I knew about you so that they could locate that money as well. Millions of dollars, Mary. Millions. What were you going to do with that?"

"Spend it. Keep it. It was mine. Mommy and I worked hard in getting it, and I wasn't going to let anyone take it from me." Mary frowned. "What do you mean, you've redeemed yourself?"

"When I died—the first time, anyway—this young woman came to see me. She told me that I could help them convict you if I wanted to go back. It wasn't even hard for me to decide. You and your mother duped me along with everyone else, and there wasn't anything I could have done to save you in my lifetime. It was a pleasure to be able to hurt you from beyond. Both you and your mother." Mary asked him how he could do that to her, his little girl. "You stopped being my little girl the moment you handed that young man a gun and told him to kill Lord Hugh and Lady Suzette. You are nothing to me now. I just came here today to see if you had any remorse for what you did."

"For what I did? Daddy, I don't think you know what they've done to me here. In addition to taking my money, they are keeping me from Hugh. I want that castle, Daddy. Now." He said nothing, and she wondered if he had left her to go and start on getting her out of here. "Daddy, when they let me go, you make sure that you stand behind me and not beside me. I don't want anyone to think that you're my father, all right? Daddy?"

Mary was confident now that things were going to go her way. Her daddy might be a fool, but he loved her and he'd make sure that Hugh came around. When her meal was brought to her, Mary decided that if it was going to be her last one in this place, they could do a good deal better than just a salad and a sandwich. But no matter how much she screamed at them to come back and get it, no one did. And she didn't get her bath things either.

"They'll learn their place." She tossed the tray out of her room and sat on the bed. This time tomorrow she'd be with Hugh and his money. Things were about to look up, finally.

~~~

The courtroom was packed. Hugh looked around and wondered if they should have rented a hall to accommodate all of the people, but didn't voice his idea. He was fucking scared out of his mind, if he was honest with himself. What if the bitch was able to convince them she really was insane?

169

"She's not." Hugh looked at Kimber when she spoke. "Mary's not insane. Not in the sense that she didn't know what she was doing. I'm pretty sure that she's known all along what she was doing. She's crazy is what she is."

"What's the difference?" She grinned at him. "This is going to be good, isn't it? I can't wait to hear what you have to say about this. Tell me, please."

"Insane…the definition is mentally ill or deranged. She's proven that she's neither of those. Yeah, a little delusional, but not insane. Crazy means she's unsound of mind. Not quite her either, but she is going to have a hearing and be tried for her crimes. Even a psychopath. I looked that one up just to be sure that I got it right, by the way." Hugh asked her what that was. He knew, but wondered how it applied to Mary. "Well, she's amoral, right? No regard for others at all if it doesn't affect her, and asocial. You know, uncaring of her fellow man. Not even you. She just wanted what you brought to her, not you yourself."

"True. Her dad asked her if she loved me at all, and she thought he was kidding her. She went as far as telling him just what you said, that it was what I could give her, not who I was."

"Which brings me to the rest of what I think she is. Her lack of remorse, on anything she's done. It's as if she expects whatever happens to not affect her at all. Not the murder of your parents, or the fact that because of her actions, my brother did what he did." Hugh thought that it was the best description of Mary he'd ever heard. "Then there is the added fact that to her, this is all going to go away and that you're going to take her back. Just so you know, that is never going to happen. I will tear her apart before I let her come near you again. You are mine."

170

"I am, body, heart, and soul." Kissing her quickly on the nose, he decided that whatever happened today, he was going to take his lovely wife on a long and very private vacation. Telling her he loved her again, they all stood as soon as the judge made his way to the dais. Mary, in orange coveralls and cuffs, was brought in a few minutes later. This might be the best thing that had happened in a very long time.

After looking over the file in front of him, the judge, Markum Brown, looked out over the courtroom. He had worked with them before on cases, so he was aware of what they did for a living. He had his own ghost too, his partner in life and death, James Swindle. Mr. Swindle had died some years ago, and often conferred with them on cases of the clients that they worked with. Markum knew this, and sometimes came to them for a little chat with his lover and friend. Today, he was all judge. And a damned fine one at that.

"Miss Manchester, it says here that you have no council. I'm pretty sure you were assigned one. I did it myself." She stood up and started to speak, but he cut her off. "A simple yes or no. Do you want me to find you council?"

"For what?"

She looked around the room when someone shouted, "Murderer."

"I have some things I'd like to get cleared up, and to make some demands. This is just stupid that I'm being treated this way. But if I have to be for now, I want to be put somewhere I can sleep at night. I guess I can stay in that room during the day, but I can't sleep well on that bed they've given me. And a private shower with my own things to bathe with."

Judge Brown leaned back in his seat. "Oh, you do, do you? And what else should we give you? A ride in a limo back and forth to this hotel of your choosing?"

171

"Oh, that would be nice too. I never thought of that. I'll add it to my list." She pulled out a piece of paper and asked for a pen. None was forthcoming, and she looked at Judge Brown. "You keep notes then. I guess I can't have a pen in here. But I want my own hotel room at night. And my things, as I've said. There is also the matter of my meals. They're not fit to eat, and I want someone to come cook for me. Fresh things, not the stuff that they serve the rest of the people. And no more women taking care of me."

"Pray tell, why not?" The room laughed slightly on that, and one look from Judge Brown had them quieting down. "What reason could you have for not wanting a woman at the jail with you?"

"Well, the women are harder to have sex with. I've had sex with them before, but I just don't care for it. And they're not as easy to bribe as men. Men just think with their dicks, and I can get what I want from them." Judge Brown just stared at her. "You have to admit that if I showed you my tits right now, I could have you doing whatever I want. A woman doesn't get that with another woman."

"And you won't with me either." Mary asked him if he was queer. "Miss Manchester, my sexual orientation has nothing to do with any of this. And as for your demands, those are not going to happen either. You're here for me to judge whether or not you are competent to stand trial. Not for you to give me a list of things you are not getting."

"When I'm lady of the castle you'll change your mind. This is not the way you treat a person of my stature." Mary turned and looked at Hugh. "Hugh, I've been about as patient as I can be over this. Get me out of this now and I'll try very hard not to punish you much. I want my things and out of this place."

172

Hugh stood up, pulling Kimber with him. Enough was enough. Looking around the room and finding his mom and dad, he looked at them as they stood with Burton, a man that they had forgiven and taken under their wing.

"My parents were the greatest people on this earth. Before I lost them to a senseless murderer that day, I took them for granted. Never told them how much I loved and needed them in my life. Nor did I ever think of the things that they did for me, little things that made me the man that I am today. They wanted me to be happy, loved, and to live a long life with a woman that I could love like they did each other. I didn't know that then. It never occurred to me that I'd not have them in my life for a very long time. It all ended that day I went there to talk to them." He looked at Mary then. "You took them from me. As surely as you're standing there, you pulled the trigger that ended their lives and that of the man that did the actual killing. You ruined the lives of Burton's family, as well as the many others there that day. And now, you stand there telling me and the other people in this room, that you want better food, nicer sleeping arrangements, as well as countless other things on your list."

"You think I didn't give things up? Christ, Hugh, do you have any idea how much I suffered staying in that hovel of a hotel that my daddy got for me? There were no servants there, and I had to wear the cheapest clothing I could find to make others think that I was dirt poor and waiting on you to come for me." She rubbed her hand over the jumpsuit she had on. "Now I'm in this thing, and all I want is for us to start our life together. Get me out of this, Hugh, now, or so help me, I'm going to make you pay."

"I don't want you." Hugh moved to the end of the line of seats he and Kimber were in. As he made his way to the back of the room to leave, Mary started screaming for him to get her out of this. Even before he made it to the aisle to leave, he knew that Kimber was going to have the last word.

"Hey, Mary. Just so you know, I'm going to leave the castle just the way it is. I'm going to have lots of children with Hugh, and when we're old and gray, we'll sit on the back lawn and laugh about how you never stood a chance." Kimber pulled him to her and kissed him long and hard before looking at Mary again. "Fuck you, bitch."

They were out in the sunshine when his parents joined them. His mom was laughing and his dad was saying how Kimber was going to be just fine as the lady of the house. Burton just stood there staring at them both.

"Tell her that I love her." Hugh told Kimber what Burton said. "I'm going to go on. Steele, he said he'd help me, and I'm ready. I won't be coming back this way any time soon."

"No. I want him to be here with me." Burton just shook his head at his sister, even though she couldn't see or hear him. "Tell him to stay, Hugh. Please? I need him here with me. Guiding me."

"You'll do just fine. Perfectly, as a matter of fact." Burton looked at him. "Love her. Love her with all that you have to give her. And then, know it's less than she deserves. I don't mean that you won't give her everything she needs or wants, but she deserves so much more. I will miss her with all my heart."

"I'll take care of her. I promise you that. And I'll love her too. Every day for the rest of my life." Burton nodded and looked at his sister as Hugh continued. "Burton, you have nothing to worry about. I promise you, she will know that I love her."

"I know that. I know that deep in my heart." He looked

at him them. "Tell her to...tell her again that I loved her, and only thought to be...I don't know, Hugh. I thought that, in my grief, I was avenging her somehow."

As he faded away, Hugh held Kimber while she cried. It was for the best, they all knew that, but that didn't lessen the pain of Kimber losing him once more. He hoped that his parents had no such plans and stayed with them forever. He didn't think he could handle them leaving him. Not again.

Chapter 12

"A box came for you." Kimber was dressed for the trial to start this morning, and was waylaid by the front doorbell ringing. Hugh looked up from his desk and asked her who it was from. "I don't know. It has your name on it. And that's it. I hope you don't mind, but I went ahead and signed for it."

"Of course I don't mind. This is your home too, you know that, right?" She did, but it still overwhelmed her a bit to think that it was. "Let's see who it's from."

The box cutter slid easily through the tape, and she stood back when he opened the first flap. As he pulled out yards and yards of brown craft paper, she wondered what this box could contain. There had been lots of boxes and crates arriving every day since they'd moved temporarily into this house. Next month they were going to England to live there for six months before coming back here for the other six.

"Ah ha." She looked over his shoulder at the books inside. They were all the same, so far as she could see, and took one when he handed it to her. "What do you think? I like the cover work. It came out nicely, don't you agree?"

"Sure." She started to hand it back to him, not having a clue who the author was. "Are you a big fan? I mean, what are there, a dozen? That is really hard core for anyone, don't you think?"

"It's me." She shook her head. "It's my pen name. Ember Moon. I thought it sounded kinda like a woman. My publisher said that men sell well, but not in erotic romance. I mean, I guess they can, but we talked it over and thought this would work for me. What do you think?"

She opened it to a random page and then looked at him. "This is about a shifter, and a woman. Why did you write about a man shifter and his mate?"

"I don't know. I mean, I just wanted to dabble in writing. It was sort of a stress reliever for me. I'd write a few lines or so, then feel better. The rest of them don't know." She nodded, thinking of the ribbing they'd give him. "Not even Drew knows, and I think, for a while yet, I'd like to keep it that way."

"Can I read it?" He pulled it from her hands. "But I want to read it. Really I do. I might be able to give you some pointers on the shifter parts."

"I would rather work out the sex scenes with you." He pulled her into his arms. "I'm already starting on the next one. It's about a bunch of dragons that save the world. What do you think about that idea?"

"I don't know any dragons." She was melting under his touches when she thought of something. Jerking his head up from her shoulder, she glared at him. "I don't know any dragons, do I?"

"Not that I'm aware of." He laughed at her. "But I think that Vinnie knows a couple. And I know that her grandmother does as well. They're nice people, from what I understand."

All she could think about was how big they were. Dragons, she decided, were one kind of shifter that she might shy away from. When Tomas knocked on the door a few minutes later, Kimber was still laughing at Hugh when he had to hide behind his desk or get caught with a thick erection.

"My lady, sir, the car has arrived. And Mr. Bennett has asked that you call him as soon as you arrive at the courthouse. He said that he has some news for you." Hugh told him they'd be right along. "Very good, sir. Oh, and Mrs. Stark said that she has something for you as well. She has found what you were searching for."

As they made their way out to the limo — parking, they'd been told, was going to be a real bitch — Hugh was telling her what he'd had Addie looking for. Kimber thought it was a wonderful idea.

"It's not for my mom." She asked him who he was looking for the ring for. "It's for you. I talked to Mom, and she said she wanted you to have it. But I never got it back from the hospital. Or anything, for that matter."

"You want me to have your mom's wedding rings? I don't…she might want you to bury them with her. Your dad gave those to her."

Hugh nodded and kissed her on the nose, and told her it was a done deal. "Besides, Mom and Dad are already buried, and they don't want me to dig them up for a ring that she wanted you to have." Kimber was touched and a little nervous about it. "Dad even had me look for his ring too. I wasn't able to see to their things, and they've been put in storage at the hospital. But after all this time, the records were lost or someone misplaced them, and I asked Addie to help me find them. I'm hoping she had some luck."

The courthouse was indeed packed. The limo driver let them out in front, and they were both bombarded with reporters and camera crews. Kimber had been warned this might happen, and she had been asked not to speak to anyone. Liam, their attorney, had told them that once you spoke to one of them, they were like sharks and would come in for the kill.

They were seated in the front of the courtroom. Lines of police were all around the room; it was thought that there would be some violence from some of the men that Mary had had dealings with. No one, it seemed, had wanted to have their names ballyhooed around after all of the things she'd done had come to play. When the room hushed, they all stood while Judge Brown came in and sat down. It had been four months since Mary had been arrested, and Kimber was glad that it was finally coming to a close.

When Mary was brought into the room, Kimber had to ask Hugh if that was her. Mary had not done well in prison. Not only was her mouth swollen, but her eye had been blackened as well. Her hair, usually so neat and pretty, looked as if someone had yanked her head hard, using her hair as the rope. And orange stripes were not flattering to her either.

"I'd like a word." Mary had been ordered twice to have a seat, but she stood there glaring at the room. "I want to say something. I have that right. I know I do."

"All right, but we're not going to put up with your shenanigans today, Miss Manchester. I have a full courtroom, and there is no more time for your antics." Judge Brown told her to proceed. "But if you make me upset with you, we'll hold these hearings with you sitting in your cell with a camera as your only companion."

"I just want to know when I get to get out of here. I'm sick to death of people telling me that I'm not going home again,

180

that my money and my business have been taken over. No one will call my Hugh and tell him that I need him. When do I get what I want?" No one said a word…the judge even looked a little shocked by her questions. "Well? I don't think it's that difficult to answer. I want out of this crap. I didn't do anything that anyone wouldn't do to have what they wanted. I wanted the castle and Hugh. I took measures to ensure that was going to happen. There were people in my way of getting what I wanted. And like anyone else would have done, I fixed the problems. So what if a few people got hurt or killed? I never did it. When are you people going to admit that you made a mistake arresting me? And if you let me go right now, I'll tell Hugh to just let it go with only some money in compensation, not everything you have like you took from me."

Judge Brown looked at them, then back at Mary. Kimber wasn't sure what he was going to say, because to her, she'd just admitted that she'd done all the things she was accused of. But when the judge shook his head and looked at Mary, she knew that whatever came next, Mary wasn't going to be any happier about it than she was going to prison.

"Miss Manchester, you know, I have no idea where to even begin with you. First of all, you refused council, is that right?" Mary told him that if Hugh didn't think she needed one, then she didn't need one. "I see. Mr. McGuire, have you in any way told Miss Manchester that she was to refuse council?"

Hugh stood up. "No, I have not, Your Honor. I have had no contact with Miss Manchester since she was arrested four months ago. There have been countless calls from her to the point where I had to change my number and also have the prison block her calls to me, but I have in no way talked to her." The judge nodded. "Your Honor, I would also like to

181

point out that Miss Manchester has had others try and contact me. Some of the guards at the prison have brought me notes from her, as well as…other things. Her panties, for instance."

"Yes, I've heard about that. And they have been dealt with, I'm told." Hugh told him that he believed they'd been fired. "As it should have been. Miss Manchester, what do you have to say for yourself now?"

"Nothing. I'm going to get out of here when you okay it. The castle will be mine, and so will Hugh. I don't care if he thinks that that animal is going to be his wife. I'll deal with her as well." Judge Brown shook his head. "You never said when I get to leave. I demand that you take these cuffs off me and let me get on with my life."

Judge Brown told her to sit down. When she only stood there, defying him with a lift of her chin, the police, four of them, came toward her and she started screaming. Once they had her cuffed to the chair and one was standing on either side of her, the trial began. Kimber had a feeling that it was going to be a very long time before this thing was behind them.

~~~

Hugh wasn't sure what to think now that Mary was going to prison. She had all but confessed what she had done to the entire courtroom. Even going so far as to tell the judge that she was going to take care of him as well when she was released. Twice Mary had turned to him, begging him to come and sit with her so they could talk about what she was going to do to the castle first — her castle, she kept calling it — until the judge ordered her removal. The rest of the day went quickly.

"Do you think she'll go to prison for good?" Hugh looked over at his mom when she joined him on the deck. "I'd like to see her fry myself, but I don't think they do that to people any more. Too bad, really. I'd pay to watch her burned at the stake, wouldn't you?"

"She hurt Kimber." His mom nodded. "And she loves the ring. I'm really glad that you reminded me about it. There were a great many other things there as well. Dad's wallet, and your watch. I'm having that cleaned, and I want to give it to our first daughter."

"No, don't do that. Give her something lovely. There are any number of things in my box at home that would be nicer. That watch was...I know that it was covered in blood. I don't want any grandchild of mine to remember me that way. How about you give her my pearls? I so loved wearing them."

Hugh told her he would, then. They both said nothing for a little while. Hugh knew that she wanted to tell him something, and he thought that he could wait her out. When his dad joined them a little while later, Kimber came out on the deck as well.

"I want you to tell Kimber something for us." Hugh told his dad that he would. "All right. Your mom and I talked yesterday, and we wanted to tell Kimber that she's the best thing that could have happened to us. Not just you — mind, I love the way she makes you nearly shine with happiness — but with us as well. She's made us...well, we were going to tell her that she made us feel alive, but that's not very good either."

Hugh told Kimber what his dad said. "Tell them that even though I never met them, that I love them very much. And think the world of them."

He reminded her that they could hear her. His dad laughed a little, and reached out and held his mom's hand. They loved each other so much that Hugh hoped that he and Kimber had that kind of relationship when they were old.

"We're ready to move on." Hugh sat up in his chair, telling

them that they couldn't do that to him. "Oh Hugh, darling, we have really overstayed our welcome. And as much as we love you, we really do want to move on."

"No, Mom." Hugh told Kimber what they were saying. "You need to be here for us. What of the children we have? You know that they can see you. They'll get to know you that way."

"I'd like that too, but that's what we talked about. We know...we feel that it would hurt us more not to be able to touch them. Hold them in our arms. Not to say we won't check in sometimes, just to see if you're doing a good job or not. But we really do want to do this before it becomes impossible for us. I'm sure I'm not saying this right." His mom turned to his dad. "You tell them. You have a better way about you."

"I think you did just fine." His dad looked at him. "You understand, don't you, son? We've done all we can do here. Our murderer has been caught. And we've made sure that you're going to be loved and taken care of. We knew you would be, but we were frightened there for a while. But...well, son, it's time."

Hugh felt his heart twist up and his eyes fill with tears. His parents had always been there for him. Loved him even after they'd been taken from him. There was no way he would have made it this far if they hadn't been there.

"I think you're right." Hugh looked at Kimber when she spoke, her eyes looking at the couple that she couldn't see. "I would hate to have to watch over someone when I knew that they were out of my reach. Loving someone is hard enough without not being able to hug, touch, or even to speak to them. I miss Burton every day, but I'm really glad that he's in a better place. And he is. I know that. Having you leave us... it breaks my heart, it really does, but I fully understand why

184

you have to do it. I know that if it were me, I'd want to do the same thing."

His dad nodded, tears rolling down his face as they were his mom's, when they both stood up, holding onto the other, Hugh went to them. Telling them goodbye was like losing them all over again. But he knew that they would be forever in his heart, and that with Kimber, he would be just fine.

Chapter 13

Seventy years, five months, and ten days later.

Pacing up and down the hallway, Steele watched the others moving about. None of the nurses or the other staff had any idea who or how many people were with them, but he did. As did Kari, his son, and daughter. Steele paused outside the little office when he heard someone coming down the hall, and resumed his walk when he didn't recognize the person.

"You're going to wear a hole in the floor." Steele grinned at Hugh as he walked with him. "Did it always seem to take this long, or are we getting old?"

They hadn't aged a day in a very long time. Steele, never a vain man, glanced at his reflection as he made his turn and started down the hall again. He looked the same as he had all those years ago when he'd met and married the love of his life. Kari hadn't aged either. She was just as beautiful as she was then...more so, he thought. All of them, the twelve of them that had started out finding justice for the dead and their wives, had given birth to immortals as well. And now this.

"I think it's taking longer because we're ready for things to go to the next level." Hugh nodded and moved out of the way when someone came at them. A ghost. Neither of them had ever liked them walking through them. "When do you suppose they'll tell us anything?"

"Never. It's the way they work it." Aster came toward him, grinning. Hugh smiled at her before continuing. "She knows something. I'd bet the farm on it."

"It's moving along nicely. You should hear from the doctors in less than an hour. And you'd better not hurt Conrad. He's a good man." Steele made no promises. "I swear, if you try to hit him again, you are really going to make me mad. He loves Bethany very much."

"She's too young." Aster only snorted at him. "Well, she is. And they're too young for this to—"

"Steele, are you fussing about Bethany again?" He looked at the love of his life and shook his head. "Aster, is he fussing about our granddaughter again?"

"She's not our granddaughter, she's our great-granddaughter, and too young to be having a baby of her own." Hugh laughed. "Don't think I don't know what you've done. This is your grandson's fault. He had to have that...that boy."

"He is a good boy, and he's my great-grandson too. By the way, I know what they're naming him, do you?" Steele had been forbidden to ask any questions about the baby or anything about him. Other than knowing that Bethany was having a boy and that everything was fine, he was to stay out of it. "You're not going to like that any better than you liked our grandchildren falling in love."

Steele growled, a habit he'd picked up from Kari. The great-granddaughter of he and Kari had gone and fallen in love with Hugh and Kimber's great-grandson. It was...well, to him it was like they were in love with family. They weren't related in any way, but still....

"She's coming now."

The doctor came down the hall sporting a grin bigger than his sister had. He wanted to hit the lot of them. They were only in their twenties, both still working in their careers, and now they were having a baby. What happened to wanting to fulfil some dream before you set out to repopulate the world?

"They'd like to see you now." Steele wanted to protest, but he was afraid to. He'd been such an ass during this whole thing that he knew he had no rights to demand anything of anyone. "Mr. Bennett? Your great-granddaughter wants to see you. If you behave."

"I can behave." He realized that he'd growled out his answer, and tried again. "I'll behave. When can we go back?"

"Not everyone, just you." He thought perhaps something was wrong, and asked. "No. Nothing out of the ordinary. They just want to see you first, before anyone else."

He nodded, still sure that he was being tricked. As he made his way back to the hallway that they'd taken Bethany to hours ago, all sorts of thoughts ran in his head. He decided that they were going to close him in this room while the rest of them saw the new baby, and he was going to have to wait. He supposed he had no one to blame but himself. But as soon as he moved into the room, he knew the real meaning of fear.

Conrad stood by the door and Bethany was in the small bed. There was no one else in the room, and he started forward. If he was honest with anyone he'd tell them that Bethany was his favorite child of all time. She looked so much like his mom and Aster that it hurt him. Going to the bed, he watched her sleep. Then he looked at Conrad when he said his name.

"She just closed her eyes." He nodded. "We wanted to talk to you. I know that you're mad at us, but we are in love."

"I know that." He did too. Steele touched his finger to Bethany's cheek, and marveled again at how much she looked like his mom. "It doesn't make it easy on me. I love her very much."

"Me too." Steele knew that too. "Will you wake her? She's been wanting to talk to you since we got here. There are things we have to tell you."

"I'm really sorry, Conrad." He felt the arms of the other man engulf him and the tears start to fill his eyes. "I guess I didn't want her to grow up. I wanted her to stay my little baby."

"Grandda?" He wiped at his tears as he turned to his great-granddaughter. Bethany smiled up at him and told him she had a surprise for him. "You're gonna love it. I hope so, anyway."

"I will. Are you all right? I'm guessing the rest of them are visiting with the baby? I know I've been sort of an ass, but if you can see your way to letting me meet him, I'll be good, I promise."

She didn't answer him, but they all turned to the doorway when it opened. The nurse coming in with the large bassinet was very business-like, and told him to back up. He did so without getting to look at the baby in the bed. When she left, Bethany was handed the baby by Conrad, and she told him to come to her.

"We knew what we were going to have almost from the very beginning. No one else knows. Not the living anyway. We've sworn everyone to keep it quiet until we were ready to tell. Conrad and I wanted you to be the first to know." Steele reached for the small bundle when she handed it to him. "Grandda, I'd like for you to meet Steele Bennett Briggs McGuire, our firstborn."

Steele felt his throat close off as he pulled the blanket down from the tiny face. And when he saw him, little Steele, he burst into tears, falling so much in love with the little man that words failed him. Then Conrad nudged him in the shoulder.

"And this is Kari Elizabeth Aster McGuire, our second child." Steele staggered slightly, never letting go of the baby in his arms as a chair was shoved under him. When he was handed the second baby, he sat there like a fool, sobbing and looking at them like he'd never seen a baby before. Then Bethany said his name again.

"And this is Hugh William James McGuire, our last baby." He held them all, the small little namesakes that he knew he'd love as much as he did their mother. When he looked at Bethany and Conrad, he knew that they were in love. He held that thought to his heart as he sat there with his great-great-grandchildren in his arms.

"You're going to need a bigger house." They didn't answer him. He knew that they were living on their own, making their own way in the world without his or anyone else's support. It was the way that they'd wanted it. Well, now things were going to change. "I'm buying you a house. And a new car. That thing you're driving isn't safe for all of you. And I'm putting money in an account for them. Each of them."

"I don't think so, but thanks for offering." He looked at Conrad sharply, thinking he was making fun of him. He'd not offered, he'd ordered. He'd ordered...he started to speak again when Conrad continued. "We're doing well, Steele. And we'll do well from now on, too. I have a good job, and we've been putting our money away. We really don't need for you to do this. We're doing well."

"I'm sorry. I truly am. Why you've done this for me I'll never know. I've not been a nice person." He held the babies tighter to him, knowing that soon he'd have to give them up. But he had to fix this with his great-grandchildren too. He had noticed that neither of them had said he was just fine. "I'd very much like to help you find a bigger home. The apartment that you're living in isn't big enough, nor is it in a safe neighborhood. You have to agree about that."

He looked at Bethany, then at Conrad. They did know what sort of place they lived in. He might not have been allowed to ask about the baby...babies, but he'd been watching the news and keeping an eye on the two of them.

"We've been putting money aside to get us a house." He knew that too. And had thought to add to the account, but Kari told him if he did, she'd make him sleep on the couch for the rest of their married life. Which she pointed out wasn't going to be long after he did that. "We might have one before they start school. But we don't want your help, Steele. It's important to us that we make do this on our own."

Steele could understand that as well. He'd been born to money, but had never let it rule him. He loved that they were willing to make sacrifices to see that they provided for their children. But he needed them safe.

"I'll loan you the money now to buy. Wait before you say no. I'll charge you interest, make sure you pay me each month, and even help you out with putting some in your account to get the extras you're going to need to have three children all at once. You know that diapers alone are going to run into the

192

thousands before this is done. And you're going to need that bigger car for the car seats and things to get them around in." When they didn't comment he felt encouraged. "I really do want to put them money in the bank for their college. I did it for the others, and I would feel badly if I didn't do this for them as well."

"Grandda, you don't think this is why we did this, do you? To get you to help us? Because it's not." He stared at her, and wondered where she'd gotten that idea. "You are the best man I know besides my own dad, and we wanted to honor you in everything you've done for this family. You may not like that we're married, but you didn't disown us, and believe it or not, we know that you only had our best interest at heart."

"I'm old." Bethany told him that he wasn't. "I am. On my next birthday I'll be ninety-five. Ninety-five years old and I don't look a day over thirty. But things are changing for me so fast, and I feel like I have no control over any of it. I hate it, and I guess I feel that if I could control one thing, I'd be better. You getting married made me realize that I have never had any control over anything. Not even myself."

"Oh, Grandda. I love you so much." He nodded and handed over one of the babies as he sat there. "Let Conrad and I talk about this, and I'll let you know. It's a big decision. But the college funds, yes, you can do that. All right?"

Standing up, he kissed her on the forehead as he handed his great-great-granddaughter to her mother and held tightly onto little Steele. His namesake. His great-great-grandson. Steele was still holding the little man when the family was finally invited in. Steele felt like a man who had been given a second chance in life, and he planned to make it work.

~~~

Aster watched her brother with the children. She had yet to talk to him about what she was planning to do, and thought now was as good a time as any. It was well past time for her to move on. He'd try to talk her into staying, but she knew that she wouldn't. He was in good hands now, and she was tired.

"Don't." Aster looked at Kari and smiled at her. "You're leaving, aren't you? You're moving on."

"Yes, I've been trying to work up to it for days, telling him I mean, but there never seemed to be the right time." Kari nodded and told her that she could understand that. "Grandda left, and then Grandma, and it never seemed right to leave him alone. I know that he has you and the others, but...."

"He's your brother." Aster told her that was right. "He loves you. And to let you know, I think he might have an idea that you're moving on. He has been antsy for months now, waiting for you to tell him. It's what's made him so cranky." Kari laughed and had the others glancing their way. "I know that everyone thinks it was the babies and all, but it was him knowing that you were leaving. And he doesn't like it."

"I have to go. I'm so tired, Kari. I love you all very much, but I want to rest." Aster had been gone from this earth for nearly eighty years, much longer than she ever lived in it. "He'll understand, won't he?"

"Yes, he'll understand, but he won't like it." Aster watched as Steele talked with Conrad about something. They had gotten closer now, she could see that. And he had yet to let the baby go for others to hold. Smiling, she told Kari that she was leaving him in good hands. "But they're not your hands."

"You're not making this easy." Kari simply laughed. "I actually thought of just leaving. Not saying anything, but leaving him. I know that he'll be hurt at me, but it will be easier for him in the long run."

"Easier for him or for you?"

Aster said nothing. Truthfully, it would have been harder just to go. When Kari drifted away from her, Aster thought of all the years that she'd watched over her brother and not spoken to him. He didn't see her, but it had broken her heart every day when he became more bitter with each passing day. Then he'd met Kari, and she knew that he was going to be all right. And he had been.

Aster moved to the wall where she knew that she could get away. She wasn't leaving him just yet, but she did need to go, if only for a few minutes. She'd not been kidding when she'd told Kari she was tired. She was well beyond that.

Hearing her name, she turned to see Steele coming toward her. Her heart broke once again for what she needed to do.

"Were you going to go without saying anything?" Shaking her head at him, she told him she was going outside. "You're leaving me, aren't you?"

"Yes." It was enough. Too much even. The single word had been harder for her than the day she'd come back. "Do you remember the day I died? The day that everything we knew came apart?"

"Like it was yesterday. Not so much what happened to our parents, but to you. That I'd run you off and you got killed. Because of me." She shook her head, like she had every time he tried to take the blame for what she'd done. "You would still be alive had I not been a prick and run you off."

"I followed you. For a little while anyway. And I knew where you were headed. I'd been there too. A week or so before that day I saw Father knocking out the security cameras. And I saw the ghost." He asked her if she'd spoken to her. "No. I was trying to save my own skin. I didn't want to...well, you remember how they were. Never wanted to hear about us. But I sent her to you. I told her that if anyone could do this, you could. It's why I let you run me off. I knew where she was going to take you."

He didn't yell at her. Not that he would, that had never been his way of doing things. But he did look at her, with all the pain she'd felt that day that she'd left him there to deal with her and the ghosts that she should have helped.

"You wouldn't have been able to do it." She started to tell him she could do anything he could. "Call Dad? You'd have not been able to do that. Nor would you have survived Mom. Not that you're not strong, because there were times when I knew that you were stronger than me, but she would have hurt you before you could have taken care of it. And the police wouldn't have been able to save you."

"They really did hate us." Steele nodded. "I'm really sorry that I left you. I wish...every day, Steele, I wish I could have been there for you. For everything."

"But you were." She shook her head, reminding him that she'd left him. "You might have left me, Aster, but you were always there for me. I knew it. It's what kept me from ending my life. I could feel you there, standing over my shoulder, telling me to straighten up my act or else. You even called me dumbass a few times."

Tears burst from her. "I did. I really did. And when you would sit and brood how your life sucked, I'd come to you and remind you of all the good you were doing."

"Yes, I felt that too. And you led me to Kari." She said that she hadn't. "Not physically, but you were there too. Every time I hurt you, I could hear you then too. Telling me that you were disappointed in me. I think that's what spurred me on to make it work with her. I can't thank you enough for that."

"I love you." He told her that he loved her as well. "I never wanted you to hurt, Steele, but like you said, I wasn't as strong as you are. You were always my rock."

"And you mine, sister dear." She wanted to hug him. Pull him into her arms just one more time before she left. "I love you so much, and I know that it's time you moved on. I don't like it, but I understand. Come here and be with me once before you go."

She didn't ask him if he was sure. She knew that he hated when the ghosts walked through him, and him giving her this opportunity meant more to her than anything he'd ever said to her before. As she took the few steps to move to him, she felt something touch her. Not sure what it was, Aster looked at Steele just before she moved into his body. But she didn't. His body was real to her, as real as she seemed to be to him.

"Oh, Steele."

Wrapping her arms around him, she felt her big brother. His warm skin, the stubble at his chin. She could feel his breath on her face, his hands as they wrapped around her. Even his height as he lifted her up in his arms and swung her around. For the first time in almost a hundred years, Aster could touch the one man she loved with all her heart. Then he kissed her on the cheek, the nose, and her forehead, telling her that he loved her and would never forget her. Even as she faded out, her body leaving this world for the next, Aster knew that he was going to be safe, that she'd done all she could. Aster told him she loved him once more as his hands dropped from her body and she left him once and for all.

Before You Go...

HELP AN AUTHOR

write a review

THANK YOU!

Share your voice and help guide other readers to these wonderful books. Even if it's only a line or two your reviews help readers discover the author's books so they can continue creating stories that you'll love. Login to your favorite retailer and leave a review. Thank you.

Kathi Barton, winner of the Pinnacle Book Achievement award as well as a best-selling author on Amazon and All Romance books, lives in Nashport, Ohio with her husband Paul. When not creating new worlds and romance, Kathi and her husband enjoy camping and going to auctions. She can also be seen at county fairs with her husband who is an artist and potter.

Her muse, a cross between Jimmy Stewart and Hugh Jackman, brings her stories to life for her readers in a way that has them coming back time and again for more. Her favorite genre is paranormal romance with a great deal of spice. You can visit Kathi online and drop her an email if you'd like. She loves hearing from her fans. aaronskiss@gmail.com.

Follow Kathi on her blog: http://kathisbartonauthor.blogspot.com/

www.ingramcontent.com/pod-product-compliance
Lightning Source LLC
Chambersburg PA
CBHW032132170626
46808CB00006B/2203